DOUBLE-BOOKED

Dedicated to my kids: Byron, Bradley, Brookelyn, and Bethany.
Thanks for brainstorming, listening, and encouraging! The Chosen Girls couldn't
have happened without your love and support.

And special thanks to Robin Crouch for living and breathing these books with me.
Ohwow, you are definitely cool frijoles, woman!

The children's group of Zondervan

www.zonderkidz.com

Double-Booked
Copyright © 2007 by G Studios, LLC

Requests for information should be addressed to:
Zonderkidz, Grand Rapids, Michigan 49530

Library of Congress Cataloging-in-Publication Data

Crouch, Cheryl, 1968-
  Double-booked / by Cheryl Crouch.
    p. cm. — (The Chosen Girls)
    Summary: Trinity, Harmony, and Melody, three friends in a rock band,
  find their relationship threatened by a snobby school clique and their own
  individual personalities, but they must unite in time to sing for a crowd that
  needs to hear what they have to say.
    ISBN-13: 978-0-310-71268-8 (softcover)
    ISBN-10: 0-310-71268-8 (softcover)
    [1. Rock musicians—Fiction. 2. Interpersonal relations—Fiction.
3. Christian life—Fiction.] I. Title.
    PZ7.C8838Dou 2007
    [Fic]—dc22
                                                                    2006023531

Editor: Bruce Nuffer
Art direction and design: Sarah Molegraaf
Interior composition: Christine Orejuela-Winkelman

Printed in the United States of America

07 08 09 10 11 12 • 7 6 5 4 3 2 1

DOUBLE-BOOKED

By Cheryl Crouch

ZONDERVAN.com/
AUTHORTRACKER
follow your favorite authors

SING

I can't find enough love — send it down ~~from above~~

Doc Wazzup from
channel 6—
   or is it channel 9?
—is coming to our
shed on Tuesday
morning. I have to
remind Mamma to
record the interview
on TV!

MELODY ROCKS!

fill my heart and ~~make~~ use me
so that ~~everyone~~ people can see

TRUTH

And this is my prayer: that your (love) may abound more and more in knowledge and depth of insight.

— Philippians 1:9

If I had my own room I would blast what I want on the stereo **ALL THE TIME!** And I could leave the light on until three a.m. if I wanted to or talk on the phone **LOUD.** I could leave clothes all over the floor and no one would gripe at me!

ADMIT ONE

The Chosen Girls
7:30 pm

Theater: **3-A**

Harmony

I love love love being on TV! Maybe someday I'll be an actress or a news reporter or a weather person...

PRAYER

CONCERT SITES:

* The Rec Center

* ~~My back yard~~

* Java Joint

* Other coffee houses?

* Community Center

* Melody's Church

* Other churches

* ?????

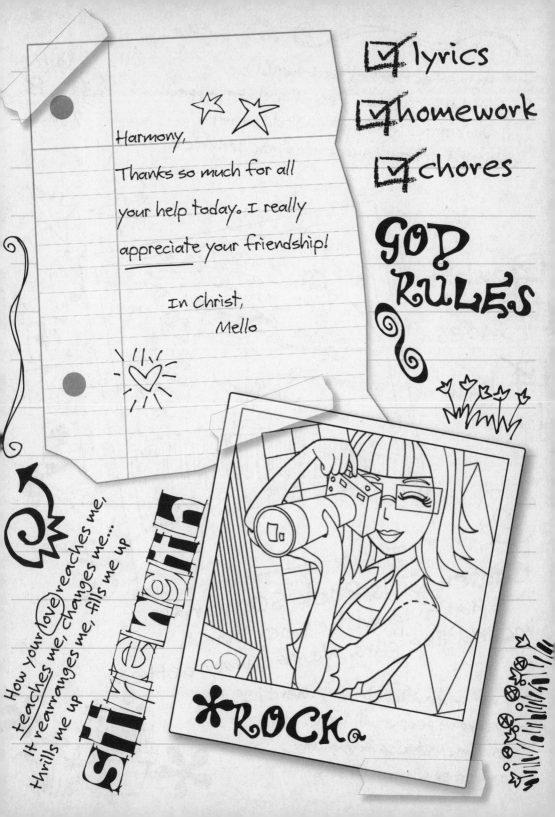

☑ lyrics
☑ homework
☑ chores

GOD RULES

Harmony,

Thanks so much for all your help today. I really appreciate your friendship!

In Christ,
Mello

strength

How your love reaches me,
teaches me, changes me.
It rearranges me, fills me up
thrills me up

ROCK

My perfect breakfast would be chocolate-chip waffles, chocolate-dipped strawberries, and hot chocolate with whipped cream (and chocolate sprinkles).

- ☑ outfit
- ☑ shoes
- ☑ hair

Chosen Girls Rock SO hard!
Makayla wishes her band rocked like ours. We are way better.

Help me spread (love) everywhere I go
so everyone people will know.
Send me ~~away~~ so far away
no matter where, I'll say...

PEACE

Hopetown's
Twentieth Annual

Fall Fling

Sunday, October 2
4 p.m. – 10 p.m.

Civic Center Park

What's up with Trin??????!?!!!???!?!

Closing Celebration for Lewisville Youth Week

Featuring THE CHOSEN GIRLS

This Saturday, 11:00 a.m.

at the Gazebo in the Park

BEST FRIENDS!

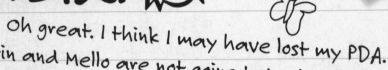

Oh great. I think I may have lost my PDA. Trin and Mello are not going to be happy with me at all. I have no idea where I put it. I must have left it somewhere. I've checked everywhere and it's nowhere to be found. I'm in so much trouble. They are going to be so mad!

ADMIT ONE

KHC
7:30 pm
. . . .
Theater: **3-A**

Harmony

chapter • 1

...

The scariest moment of my life? My first time in the James Moore cafeteria.

I searched frantically for an amiga.

I practically heard the clock on the wall ticking. I could only stand there holding my tray for so long.

I didn't dare sit next to the windows. I'm not an outcast, but I'm not one of the Snob Mob, either.

I finally spotted some girl I remembered from third grade. I walked over, said "Hi, I'm Harmony," and sat down. She didn't even smile, but it beat sitting alone.

Anyway, all that happened ages ago.

This year my best friend Mello is in my lunch. So is our new friend, Trin, who moved here this summer.

We're not sitting by the windows or anything, but becoming rock stars and superheroes over the summer didn't hurt us any.

So, I'm thinking this is going to be the best year of my life—if Trin and Mello don't drive each other loco …

• • •

I played a repeating pattern on my bass guitar while we waited in the shed for the TV film crew.

"Cool frijoles!" I said. "I'm so pumped. I set the DVR to record channel 9 already, just in case they come early."

"Channel 9?" Mello asked, dropping her drumsticks. "I thought Doc Wazzup was on channel 6. My parents are recording channel 6!"

"Run! Tell them to change it," Trin yelled.

"Fine," Mello snapped. "Just don't be so bossy in front of the TV guys."

Even though Mello's house is only fifty feet away from the shed where we practice, it made me nervous to see her heading out the door.

"Uno momento," I cried. "Use my cell. He could be here any minute."

Mello made the call, tossed my phone back, and flounced onto her big tan couch, separated from Trin by a pile of throw pillows.

"I am definitely not excited about this," Mello said. "I wish we could just get it over with." Then, for the third time, she asked, "What time is it?"

"It's two minutes since the last time you asked," Trin answered, whapping Mello's shoulder with a pillow. "Raise your hand if you think Mello is the only person in the world who doesn't want to be on TV. Ohwow, I can't believe Doc Wazzup is coming to the shed! Is my hair OK?"

"Definitely," Mello answered. "It's still pink and perfect, just like the last time you asked—two minutes ago!"

I actually felt glad to see Lamont appear in the doorway. Mello and I used to send her next-door neighbor away, but those days were as ancient history as elementary school.

"What about mine?" Lamont asked, rubbing his black curly hair, so short you could almost see his scalp. "I didn't have time to do much with my hair today."

Trin threw the pillow at him with a hard overhand, but Lamont ducked, and the ocean-blue missile sailed above his head.

It smacked Doc Wazzup right in the face. I almost dropped my guitar.

Our famous guest took a step back and put his hands up like a shield in front of him. "Hold your fire," he said. "Is it safe to come in?"

"Ohwow, I'm so sorry," Trin answered. "I didn't mean to hit you in the face. I mean, I didn't mean to hit you at all. I meant to hit ... Ohwow." She hid her face in her hands.

I elbowed Lamont out of the way and held out one hand to the TV host. He didn't look much taller than me. I looked into his bright blue eyes and said, "Welcome to the shed. I'm Harmony—a big fan of yours."

He smiled and shook my hand.

Doc didn't look like a TV news anchor. He didn't have a million-dollar smile. (His teeth were a little crooked.) He didn't have slick black hair. (His was light brown and a little messy.) He looked more like somebody's big brother.

I thought, *That's why everyone loves him.*

I heard someone on the driveway call, "I take it we finally found the right place. Where do we set up, Dan?"

Doc Wazzup turned around and called, "Come on inside."

Lamont and I got out of the way. Doc was followed by a tall, blonde woman and a short, bald man with a bunch of equipment. They had headsets on and looked very official.

The woman looked around and smiled. "Nice place. Who did your decorating?"

Mello lit up like a Christmas tree, but she didn't say anything.

I pointed to her. "Mello did it all by herself."

Lamont started coughing and sputtering until Mello finally said, "Lamont helped a little."

He shrugged. "Just a few touches here and there. Nothing major."

The crew set up equipment. The man erected huge bright lights on tall silver poles. The woman worked on a little sound system and a computer monitor. They kept running in and out, bringing in more stuff and more extension cords. Every couple of minutes the bald man would yell.

"Twelve minutes!"

"Ten minutes!"

"Eight minutes!"

Meanwhile, Doc Wazzup talked to us. "My name is Dan Miller. Doc Wazzup is kind of a stage name I use for these interviews."

I nodded like I knew that all along.

He told us to get in place with our instruments, and he showed Lamont where to sit on the edge of the couch. He said to go with the flow and act natural.

Mello tripped on the way to her stool, and she fell into her drum set, making so much noise that I jumped and the tall blonde screamed.

"Hey, you said to act natural," Lamont said with a smirk. "Tripping is as natural for Mello as it gets."

Mello stuck her tongue out at him and sat down.

The bald man said, "This is live, so we only get one shot at it. Lela will count down with her fingers when we're ready."

The bald man pointed the camera at us, and Mello tapped on her legs. Trin wound her hair around her finger. I tried to signal them to relax.

Then Mello looked at me and pulled on her ear. She doesn't usually pull on her ear when she's nervous. *How weird.* I'm the one who pulls on my —

Oh. I let go of my ear, adjusted my glasses, and put my hands in my lap.

"One minute!"

I realized that I really needed to go to the bathroom.

"Thirty seconds!"

Oh, well.

Lela stared at the monitor. She held up her hand. Three fingers. Two fingers. One finger.

The camera light glowed red.

Doc — or Dan — smiled into the camera. "Hello, Los Angeles! Doc Wazzup coming to you live and on location from the . . . " He looked around the shed. "From the back-yard recording studio of the hottest new teen group in Southern California: the Chosen Girls. And we're here to find out, wazzup?"

He reached his mike out to Trin. "Introduce yourself."

Trin turned on her movie star smile. "I'm Trin Adams."

"And you play …?"

She held her guitar up a little. "I play electric guitar and sing lead."

He rubbed his nose, looked at the camera, and said, "She also throws a mean pillow."

Trin turned bright red. I choked back my laughter because I knew it would make me snort, but Mello cracked up.

"Could I try a lick on your guitar, Trin?" Doc asked.

"Sure." She handed it over.

He struck a rock star pose and said, "I always wanted to be in a band." He played a couple really bad notes and said, "Anytime Trin is sick, you can call me." He handed back the instrument as he pointed the mike toward me. "And you are …?"

My throat felt dry, and my head pounded louder than Mello's bass drum. *Pretend it's just Lamont filming again.* I looked right at the camera and said, "I'm Harmony Gomez. I play bass guitar."

"Play something, Harmony," he said.

I repeated my favorite bass line, and he did some scary dance moves (like a rapper doing ballet) that made everyone laugh again.

"And on drums we have …" he stuck the mike under Mello's mouth. I half expected her to hide under her drum set, but she sat up and smiled. "I'm Melody McMann."

"Will you let me play your drums?" he asked.

She nodded.

"Any tips?" he asked as he took her place on the stool.

She shook her head. "Just have fun."

He tapped the edge of a snare and yelled, "One. Two. Three. Four." And then he went crazy. Bass, high hat, snares, toms—he must have hit all of them four times each in about ten seconds.

He stopped and said, "Oh, yeah! So, Mello, tell me how you girls started your band."

Mello? I thought. *She didn't even want to be on TV. Why did he pick her for the good question?*

She said, "Trin found out there was a music video contest. She and Harmony wanted to enter. They talked me into it."

Doc laughed. "So you didn't want to do it at first?"

Mello said, "No. I don't like being in front of people."

"So you probably weren't too excited about this live interview with me, were you?"

Mello's turn to go red.

He laughed again. "It's OK. I won't take it personally." He turned to Trin. "So, Trin, part of what made your video entry special is who made it. Can you tell me about that?"

Trin said, "Our friend Lamont Williams did our video."

The bald guy swung the camera toward Lamont. Lamont waved.

Doc said, "I've seen the video you made. It's amazing. You turned these girls into superheroes. How did you do that?"

Lamont said, "I used my laptop and some video editing software. I also used some free graphics I downloaded. With computer graphics, the hardest thing is—"

"Whoa, there, Lamont. Don't give away all your secrets." Doc faced me again. "So, Harmony, what's the best thing about the Chosen Girls?"

Crud. He asked me the hardest question. I have to say something brilliant and make our band stand out. This could be the defining moment for us—our chance to catch some agent's eye.

I stared at the blinking light on the camera. It kind of hypnotized me.

"I guess there are so many good things, it's hard to narrow it down, huh?" Doc prompted.

Come on! I begged myself. *Say something. Anything!*

Finally, I had a thought. "I think the best part is that we aren't just a band. We're best friends."

"How great is that?" Doc said. "On that note, I'm going to let these musicians play a song for you. I hope they do okay without my help. This has been Doc Wazzup — live and on location — and these are the Chosen Girls."

He pointed to us, and Mello tapped four beats. Then she and I started in. On the third measure, Trin joined in on electric. Trin sang, and Mello echoed. It sounded awesome. We got halfway through the chorus when the light on the camera went out and the tall lady said, "Cut."

We stopped. Trin asked, "What's wrong?"

My face felt hot. "Did we mess up?"

"No. Nothing's wrong. You sounded great. That's just all we had time for. The network cut to a commercial," she explained.

Doc Wazzup walked around bonking fists with us. "So I guess you have to get to school now, huh?" he asked.

I groaned.

A live TV interview . . . cool frijoles.

Being in a rock band with my best friends . . . incredible.

Another day of school . . . boring.

It didn't take long to find out I was wrong about that.

chapter • 2

...

Later Tuesday Morning

We finished shooting at 6:35 a.m. At 6:45, I burst into my house, ready for everyone to mob me—the big star.

The house was silent.

Our house is never silent.

"I'm home!" I yelled, dropping my guitar onto the couch. Nothing. I tried again. "*Hola!*"

Mamma came rushing out of the hall. "Hush! I just got MaraCruz back to sleep."

"Oh!" I said, smiling. "Did you wake her up to watch me on TV? What did she say?" I imagined my three-year-old sister pointing at the screen and yelling, "Hominy! Hominy!"

Mamma shook her head. "No, I didn't wake her. She woke up sick and started throwing up right after you left."

"So she didn't get to see my interview?" I asked.

"No, Harmony. To tell the truth, I barely saw it." She smiled and clasped her hands together. "So how did it go?"

I shrugged. I wanted Mamma to tell me how it went, not ask me how it went. *"You were stunning, Harmony! I've never seen a prettier girl. And so quick with your brilliant answer. The band sounded incredible ..."*

"I don't know," I mumbled. "OK, I think. What did Richie say?"

Mamma hugged me. In a soft voice she said, "I didn't wake him up, *hija*. You know how he gets when he doesn't get enough sleep. But I think Julia watched."

Just then my older sister came into the family room, running a brush through her hair as she walked. I looked at her expectantly.

"Mamma, I have to work after school today. Can I take the car, or do you want to drop me off?" she asked. She pulled her long hair into a ponytail.

"I'd rather drop you off," Mamma answered. "I might need the car later."

Julia did what I call the huffy-puffy. She took a big breath and let it out real loud, and her shoulders drooped. "Can I drive, though?" she asked. She just got her license, so now her life revolves around driving. That and what she calls having a "real" job at the grocery.

Mamma smiled at her. She said, "Yes, you can drive."

Julia smiled, already over her little tantrum. "Thanks, Mamma."

I didn't think I should have to ask about my TV appearance, but apparently no one else planned to bring it up. I said, "So, what did you think of Doc Wazzup today?"

"Oh, yeah," Julia answered. "Good job on 'we're not just a band, we're best friends too.' You're a natural, Harmony." She chucked me on the shoulder and said, "I'll start breakfast, Mamma." Then she went into the kitchen, and I could hear her getting out dishes.

"Are you hungry?" Mamma asked me.

I did feel hungry, but not for breakfast. I felt hungry for a little more attention. I just got interviewed on live TV. Didn't someone want to ask me what it was like? Or how Doc Wazzup acted with the cameras off? Whether I felt nervous?

"Nah, I'm not hungry," I answered Mamma, flipping the TV to channel 3. "But I want to be sure the recording worked. I want to send a copy to Tony at college. And Papi can see it when he gets back. When will he be home?"

"He had an overnight in Phoenix last night, and he flies all day today," Mamma answered as she headed to the kitchen. "He's hoping to be home around eight."

I rewound the tape. I hated it that Papi missed the show. I know being an air marshal is important, but sometimes—like today or when he misses my birthday—I wish someone else could keep the airplanes safe.

At least it gave me an excuse to watch the video. I pushed play.

I saw news reporters, but not the ones from channel 9. "Mamma, did anyone mess with the TV?"

Mamma came back in. "Harmony, please don't wake up MaraCruz and Richie. I'm the only person who touched the TV. I noticed you had it set for the wrong channel, so I switched it," she answered.

My turn to do the huffy-puffy. "Mamma, I had it set exactly right to record. You made it record a different channel."

"Oh, no! I'm sorry, *hija*," she said. "Maybe we can get a copy. I bet Mello's parents recorded it."

Yeah, I bet they did, I thought. *And they're probably both sitting on the couch with her right now, watching it, asking her questions, and telling her how amazing she is.*

Mello is an only child. She had an older brother, but he died in a car wreck back when we were seven. It's not that I want something to happen to my brothers or sisters. I love them all. But is it too much to ask that they choose a different time to vomit or sleep or worry about driving and cooking breakfast? Would it be so awful if for once I knew how it felt to be the center of attention?

• • •

Trin and Mello were just what I needed. On our way to school in the McMann-mobile, we talked over every detail of the interview.

"It seems like someone should carry our book bags for us, don't you think? Now that we're TV stars and all," I said as we got out of the car.

Mello laughed as we crossed the parking lot. "We aren't stars, Harmony. We've only been on TV twice. Besides, your bag has wheels."

"It's way more than twice if you count every time they play our video. It's on all the time," Trin pointed out. We stepped onto the sidewalk in front of the school. "I'm with Harmony. Maybe if we get really famous, we won't have to go to school at all."

"*Oh, yeah!*" I said. "What do we have to do to get that famous?"

Trin shrugged. We reached the bottom of the stairs and stopped. "I think we'd have to do concerts and CDs and stuff. Maybe get a manager."

"Oh, wow," I said, my heart already beating faster. I remembered how it felt at the award ceremony—all those people rocking to our music. "I can see us on stage in front of hundreds of people—"

"I can't, and I don't want to," Mello interrupted, dropping her bag and crossing her arms. "Harmony, you promised me we would never do live concerts."

"I promised?" I asked. "When did we talk about concerts?"

Mello looked away, so I turned to Trin.

"Don't you think it would be fun to do concerts, Trin?"

"Ohwow, yes!" she answered. She looked at her watch. "Enough dreaming, though. It's almost time for the bell."

We picked up our stuff, and I smiled at Mello. She didn't smile back. I strapped my bag on my back so I could link one arm through hers. I held my other elbow out to Trin, and she slid her arm through. We started up the crowded concrete steps that lead to the front door of the school.

Halfway up, a short, brown-haired boy said, "Hey, it's the Chosen Girls! I saw them on Doc Wazzup this morning."

Cool frijoles!

I flashed a huge smile. I thought he might want an autograph. Mello turned to smile too, and then suddenly all three of us fell into a heap.

All I can figure is Mello tripped. Since our elbows were locked together, when she went down she pulled me down on top of her, and I pulled Trin down on top of me.

I expected Mello to cry or something. But she just giggled and said, "At least this won't be on TV."

I started snorting and felt stuff shooting out of my nose. A lot of stuff. *No es bueno.*

Trin, our new best buddy, untangled herself and walked on up the steps. Like she had no idea who we were!

Mello stopped laughing and said, "What's that about?"

"Hasn't Trin heard of loyalty?" I asked. "You never leave me when I shoot snot out of my nose."

Mello giggled again and said, "And when I fall, you fall with me."

Mello and I scrambled up, and I dug for a tissue. I hoped not too many people saw our big spill. I looked around and ...

I wanted to die. Because four steps down stood Makayla, Bailey, Ella, and Jamie. The entire Snob Mob.

"Did you have a nice trip?" Makayla asked in a voice loud enough to reach Death Valley.

She poked Bailey, her biggest fan. Bailey said, "See ya next fall!" and they pranced past us, laughing their loud, explosive laughs.

I turned to Mello and said, "Wow. Not everyone can laugh that hard at a joke that old."

At least Cole Baker—the cutest boy at James Moore— and his friends weren't on the steps. My right ankle hurt, but no way would I limp as I headed for the door. I clenched my teeth and trudged up.

I made it to the top before I realized why Cole and his friends weren't on the steps. They were waiting by the front door.

Watching the whole thing.

It didn't even help when Cole waved his cool little two-finger "I see you but I'm acting like I don't see you" wave. Ugh. I could feel my face flushing.

At that moment the bell rang. Isn't there a saying about "the bell is a savior" or "saved by the bell" or something? I understood it for the first time that day.

I ran into the science room, and Sidney yelled, "Hey, I saw you on Doc Wazzup this morning!"

I hardly knew Sidney, but I decided right then to love her forever. Instead of being the girl who just fell, I became the TV star.

"You were on TV?" Trenton asked.

"I saw it. Your music video is incredible!" Lizzie said.

I could hear Makayla's voice in the back of the room. "Doc Wazzup is about as stupid as he is ugly." And, "He obviously doesn't know much about music, if he picked the Chosen Girls to interview."

I ignored Makayla and answered everyone's questions about the band.

"Weren't you nervous?" Sidney asked me. "You didn't look scared at all."

I fluffed the ends of my hair and said, "*Sí*, before the camera came on I was a little scared. But once we started, I just had a good time. My sister says I'm a natural."

I heard, "All right, class." I looked up. I hadn't even noticed we had a substitute.

"I'm Mr. Brown," he said. "Mr. Schmidt is sick today, and I will be your teacher. We'll begin with roll call."

Argh. I knew what that meant. Sure enough, after he called Becca Fellers, it happened.

"I'm probably not going to get this right," he said. "Is it … Ammonia Gomez?" He pronounced my real first name, Armonia, like ammonia, the stuff *mi abuela* cleaned toilets with back in Peru.

A familiar laugh filled the room. "I think she prefers Harmonica, Mr. Brown," Makayla said.

I took a deep breath and said, "Actually, Mr. Brown, it's pronounced *Ar-mo-nee-ah*. It's Spanish for *Harmony*, which is what I go by."

Mr. Brown smiled at me. "You have a beautiful name, Harmony," he said. Then he went on with roll call.

I spent the rest of science imagining sold-out concerts, screaming fans, and TV interviews. I thought, *When our band is big-time famous, Makayla will have to shut her mouth. And I'm going to make it happen — soon.*

chapter • 3

...

Still Tuesday

I grabbed a sloppy joe from the hot lunch line and headed straight for Trin and Mello. Before I even sat down, I blurted out my great idea. "I'll be our band manager!" I plopped my tray on the table in front of Mello.

Mello's fork froze halfway to her mouth. "And manage what?" she asked, her eyes narrowing.

"Raise your hand if you think it's perfect!" Trin said, ignoring Mello. "You can do it until we get rich and famous, and then we can pay some big shot to handle everything. Just don't schedule anything for this first semester."

"Are you loco?" I asked. "We'll be old women by Christmas. Washed up. Forgotten. We need to starch while the iron is hot!"

I sat down, bowed my head for a quick prayer, and then took a big bite of sloppy joe.

"It's *strike* while the iron is hot, Harmony. Not *starch*. But you can forget it, because there's nothing to strike," Mello insisted. "We won the contest. Our video is on TV. I admit I had fun, but it was a one-time deal. End of story." She finally put the bite of salad in her mouth.

Trin sighed and pointed a carrot stick at Mello. "You don't get it, do you? The contest was the beginning, not the end. We have a mission! The Chosen Girls are going to be huge."

"Actually, Trin, *you* don't get it," Mello said, jabbing the air with her fork. "You are not in charge of my life."

"Of course, Mello," I said, determined to keep the peace. "But I totally agree with Trin about our band having a mission."

"But not right now," Trin continued. "Be real, Harmony. I'm trying to get used to a new school and a new ballet studio. I can't make the band a priority yet."

I thought, *Yeah, we saw that on the stairs this morning.*

I wanted to ask why she left us on the steps, but I didn't want to make Trin or Mello mad. I decided to change the subject. "Everyone's talking about Doc Wazzup today." Then I lowered my voice and leaned forward. "Makayla fumed all through science." I grinned as I coated a french fry with ketchup.

Trin nodded. "You can't blame her. Is it fair that we get all the attention? I mean, her band got first place in the youth category, but they haven't been on the news or anything."

"I'm surprised her dad hasn't paid the TV station to do a story about her band," Mello said. "I don't feel sorry for her at all."

Trin insisted, "They easily could have won best overall. Then how would we feel?"

"No way," I said. "We had the grand prize hands up."

Mello giggled. "It's hands *down*, Harmony."

•••

After lunch, Mello and I walked to yearbook together.

"Why did Trin stand up for Makayla's band?" Mello asked as we pushed through the crowded halls. "It's almost like she wishes she were one of them instead of one of us."

"No way," I said, trying to sound more sure than I felt. "She just hasn't been around them forever like we have, Mello." I tried to think of something else to talk about. "I'm psyched we both made yearbook."

"Definitely. Mrs. Gates rocks," Mello said.

"Yeah," I agreed. "She likes us. I hope she'll let me be a photographer."

"Not me," Mello said, shaking her head. "I'd much rather sit at a computer and do layouts."

We went into the classroom and found seats next to each other at one of the large tables.

Mrs. Gates smiled at the class and said, "Are any of you curious about what your position on the staff will be this year?"

Everyone shifted around excitedly.

I said, "Sí!"

Mello said, "Definitely."

"Well, I'm going to tell you," she said. Then her lips tightened mischievously, and she added, "tomorrow."

•••

I heaved a sigh of relief as I dropped my book bag on the gym floor. I dug around in it until I found my PE clothes, then grabbed them and rushed into the locker room.

I wove through other students and finally found Trin on a bench, already dressed and tying her sneakers. She said, "Hey, Harmony! How's our new band manager?"

"Mrs. Burledge held us late in English again," I said, breathing hard. "That drives me loco. Of course she won't give excuse slips, so I have to run to make it here before the bell rings." I flopped down on the bench. "I feel like I've already had PE!"

"At least we're still doing bowling today," Trin reminded me. "It's easy."

I rolled my eyes as I slipped off my sandals. "I'm really a rotten bowler. You just can't tell it with these fake lanes Coach set up in the gym. It's impossible to miss, since there aren't any gutters. I wonder how she thought of trying to bowl in a basketball gym."

"Don't gripe. It beats running the mile," Trin said. Then out of the blue she asked, "Harmony, what's Mello's deal? Why does she spaz about doing stuff in front of people?"

"I don't know," I answered, jamming my feet into white socks. "She's always been that way, and I don't get it. Like with the band—we have this amazing opportunity, and she doesn't even care. She acts like it's a big burden."

I poked my head through the neck of my T-shirt and smiled at Trin. "I'm glad you moved here," I told her. "You get me."

I pulled on my shorts, and we headed for the gym. Trin said, "Thanks. But raise your hand if you can't understand how you and Mello have been friends so long. You're total opposites."

I thought about it. Mello's shy and quiet, and I'm loud and outgoing. Mello likes simple styles, and I like bright, bold stuff. Still, Mello has been like a sister to me since second grade. I hoped Trin didn't think that was going to change.

We got our plastic bowling balls. They're like the toy ones we played with as kids, but bigger and heavier. Next we found a lane in the gym. Makayla and her Snob Mob took the lane next to ours. Not a good sign.

Before we began, Coach Howland taught about bowling etiquette. She talked about always waiting for the bowler on your right, and stuff like that.

I giggled and whispered to Trin, "I didn't know you had to have good manners to bowl." I pretended to take a sip from a tea cup, holding my pinky up. Then I said, "I believe it's your turn to bowl, Madam."

Trin covered her mouth and answered, "Oh, no, my dear, won't you please preceed me?"

Right away, Makayla got her ball and walked to the beginning of her lane. She stood there like she was ready to bowl, but first she flipped her short silvery-blonde hair from side to side and looked around to make sure everyone saw her.

Then, in a very nasally voice, she started singing, "Oh, make me strong. This lane is long. Sometimes I feel like I will fall." She staggered, as if the plastic bowling ball weighed fifty pounds, and made a cheesy scared face. Then she fell down and started laughing. Bailey, Ella, and Jamie laughed so hard they turned red and wiped tears from their faces.

The other people in class laughed too, but I don't think they knew what they were laughing at. They didn't know Makayla's whole song was for Trin and me.

I looked at Trin in shock. "You've Chosen Me" is the song we sang in the video contest. It was just like Makayla to make up fake words to it and turn it into a joke. But she didn't just hurt our feelings. That song is kind of a prayer. So it was like Makayla was making fun of God.

Trin just shrugged and whispered, "What do you expect?"

I ignored them, walked up, and bowled. I actually knocked down seven pins. I high-fived Trin and took my second turn before Makayla calmed down enough to bowl.

The peace didn't last long. Bailey took over. She sang part of the chorus to our song, which is supposed to say, "And in my soul, the words you speak, they set me free to hope, to dream, to really breathe." Instead, she struck a pose like a singing diva. She belted out, "And in my soul, the words you speak, they let me know I am a geek."

If Makayla could've laughed any harder, someone might have dialed 9-1-1. Kids three and four lanes down laughed along with her.

Trin stood up and walked to our lane. I could tell she had a plan, and I felt nervous. I never know what to expect from Trin.

Facing the pins, she looked up to heaven and sang in her rich, crystal-clear voice, "Show me your face. I need your grace to be the person you have called." It seemed way obvious why she needed God's grace—to deal with someone as rude as Makayla.

The other kids in class got quiet and looked around like they didn't know what to do. Trin wasn't laughing, so her singing didn't seem like part of the joke. But people don't just sing to God in the middle of a PE lesson on bowling either. At least, they didn't before Trin moved to Hopetown.

That's why I love Trin. She is herself, and she doesn't care what anybody thinks.

A redheaded girl two lanes over said, "Wow! She can sing."

Another girl said, "Sing some more!"

But Trin didn't even turn around. She sent her bowling ball rolling toward the pins—and got a strike. She yelled, "Sweet!"

Everyone who had been watching cheered.

Trin turned around and smiled, then walked back to where I stood.

If she meant to shock the Snob Mob, it worked. They pretty much kept their mouths shut for the rest of PE, but I kept replaying Makayla's song in my head until I felt crazy-angry about it.

When PE ended and Trin started talking to Ella, I couldn't believe it. I don't know what she talked about, because I didn't want to get closer to any snobs than I had to. It must have been pretty interesting, because while I watched, they walked out of class together.

For the second time in one day, Trin walked off and left me.

chapter • 4

...

"Mello, isn't there at least some little part of you that wants to make it big?" I asked that afternoon in the shed.

She kept playing her drums and said, "Define 'make it big.'"

I plucked a few notes on my bass guitar and looked around. "Well, wouldn't it be cool frijoles to jam in a studio, instead of some old garage?"

Mello put her sticks down. "So now the shed is 'some old garage'?" she asked. She stood up and pointed to the door. "Go find yourself a studio, then. But this 'old garage' has worked for us since second grade, and I'm staying here."

"Whoa, Mello!" I put down my bass and walked to her drum set. I picked up her sticks and held them out to her. "I'm sorry. I love the shed—especially since you redid it. It's awesome."

She took the sticks. I went back to my guitar. "How about I'll shut my mouth and we'll just jam. Let's play for fun, like we used to."

Mello smiled. "Before we were rock stars and superheroes?"

"Yeah," I answered. "I want to pull out all the stamps."

"You mean 'pull out all the *stops*'?" she asked.

"I guess," I agreed. "I don't really know what it means."

"Neither do I," she admitted. "I think it means you go for it. Give it everything you've got."

"Sí! That's exactly what I want to do. Come on!"

I started in on my favorite bass pattern.

Mello joined in. *Boom, boom, thump. Boom, thump.*

We kept getting louder and more intense.

I let the music take over, and I played the most awesome riff. It ended in an intense low note.

I felt it more than heard it. The walls of the shed shook. One of Mello's flower pictures actually fell down!

"Cool frijoles!" I yelled. "I've never knocked anything down with music before. We totally rock!"

Mello dropped her drumsticks and said, "My botanical print!" She ran to it.

I danced around with my guitar. "I made a picture fall! I make powerful music! This is serious jamming!"

Mello said, "Yeah, you didn't pay for this print out of your own allowance."

She knelt on the floor with the framed print in her hands.

"I'm sorry, Mello. It didn't break or anything, did it?"

She turned it around. I could see a big crack that went from one corner of the glass to the other.

"Oh. No es bueno. I really am sorry, Mello."

She looked up at me with a blotchy face. "Oh, I know you didn't mean to break it, Harmony. But you always get so into stuff that you don't think." Then she turned red, like she hadn't meant to say that.

"What do you mean?" I asked.

She shrugged. "You just always have to be the best: straight As, winning every karate match, grand overall in the video contest."

I laughed. "You are so wrong, Mello. I'm never the best." I propped my guitar against the stand and sat down on the couch. "I get good grades, but someone always does better. I win matches at karate, but I never win the whole tournament."

I thought about that morning at my house. I leaned forward and cupped my chin in my hands. "I'm not even the best at anything in *mi familia*. I have a big brother in college and a big sister who drives and has a job. I have a little brother who makes everyone laugh and a little sister everyone thinks is adorable. Then there's me." I stopped to sigh. "I'm too young to work or drive, and I'm too old to be silly or adorable." I looked at Mello, who finally stood up. "I've never been the best at anything until the Chosen Girls," I said. "Standing on stage with all those people cheering for us — I loved it! I thought you did too."

Mello smiled. "Yeah, it was much cooler than I thought it'd be."

"So come on!" I said. "We can do more. Our band can be huge!"

"You're doing it *again*, Harmony," she said.

I stood up. "Sorry."

We hung the picture back up, crack and all.

"I'll buy new glass for it," I offered. "Or, if you want, we can leave it. Then it will always remind us of the most awesome riff I ever—"

Mello kind of growled, and her eyes narrowed into little angry slits.

"Sí," I said, nodding. "I'll buy the glass."

Mello sighed. "Let's stop. I've still got two chapters to read in English and half a problem set in math."

"Yeah. This isn't exactly working like I planned, anyway," I mumbled.

Mello tilted her head to one side. "What do you mean, like you planned?"

Oops! I hadn't meant to admit that. "I just mean, I hurt your feelings about the shed, and then I broke your picture." I started putting my bass away. "I'm sorry."

Mello said, "No worries." She walked to the door and added, "This was fun, and I don't think we've been by ourselves since school started. Trin is great, but she always takes over."

"She sure wasn't impressed with us on the stairs this morning," I added.

Mello nodded and said, "Well, now that we're finished with the band, you and I can hang more often."

"Sí, sure," I answered. Mello went in her house, and I started up the hill.

Mello just didn't get it. And Trin . . . did she even want to be a Chosen Girl anymore?

I needed to chat this out with someone, so I turned around and walked to Lamont's front door and knocked.

His little sister, Pashay, came to the door. "Hey, Harmony."

I glanced over at Mello's house. I would die if she knew I'd gone looking for Lamont. I hoped the clump of palm trees hid me from view. "Can I come in?" I asked.

"Sure," she answered. "What's up?"

"I need to talk to Lamont," I said. Lamont is a geek that Mello and I have tolerated over the years, but since he made our music video, he's moved up a notch.

I figured since he was part of our band's success, he would understand my frustration.

Pashay led me into the family room and went to get her brother.

Lamont bounded in on his long skinny legs and said, "Hey, Harmony. You look weird without Mello."

"*Gracias*, Lamont," I answered. "You always make me feel so special."

He plopped into an overstuffed chair and said, "What's up?"

I put my bass down, sat on the edge of a chair across from him, and said, "I need to talk to someone about the Chosen Girls. I think we've got what it takes to be famous."

He stretched his long arms up, wove his fingers together, and then put his hands behind his head. "Famous, huh?" he asked with a grin.

I smiled an encouraging smile. "We practically are already, thanks to the incredible job you did on our video. Everyone who sees it loves it."

He sat straight up and pointed at me. "You know that's right! And they should. It's an amazing video. So ... I sense there is a problem."

I threw my hands up. "If only there were just one," I said. "All we have is problems. Mello doesn't want to perform in public—she might as well quit the band. And Trin is so busy with school and ballet that she won't make the Chosen Girls a priority."

I paused to give him a chance to say something inspiring. He didn't.

"So, can you help me? *Por favor*?" I finally asked.

"Help you what?"

"Help me motivate them. How can I get them to buy into the dream?"

He shook his head. "Think about what you're saying, Harmony. People are usually more motivated when it's their own dream. This is just your deal."

I jumped up and almost hugged him. Thankfully, I stopped in time. I gave him a high five instead. "Lamont, you're exactly right. Cool frijoles!"

He stood up and squinted down at me. "Uh ... I'm not sure why you're so happy about what I said."

"Because it's true," I answered. "I have to make Trin and Mello think it's their dream." I looked into his eyes. "Any hints on how to do that?"

"Rewind, Harmony!" Lamont said, shaking his head. "That is not what I said at all. You are headed for serious trouble."

I laughed as I grabbed my guitar and headed for the front door. "Lamont, you are so wrong. I am not headed for serious trouble. I am headed for serious fame."

• • •

I walked in the front door and saw Mamma, MaraCruz, and Richie already at the dinner table. Whoops.

Mamma said, "Harmony, you're late. You have fifteen minutes to eat dinner and change into your gi. It's almost time for karate."

Argh. I wanted to spend the evening dreaming about the band, not doing kicking drills and forms.

I put my case down and flopped into a chair at the table. I thought hard as I loaded my plate. I said, "I wish I could be here when Papi gets home tonight. I want to tell him about Doc Wazzup."

Mamma sighed. "Your papi called. He's stuck in New York tonight."

"He's not coming home?" Richie asked.

Mamma tousled his hair. "Tomorrow, *hijo*," she said.

MaraCruz stuck her lower lip out. "I want Papi," she whined.

I felt the same way. I shouldn't admit it because I'm practically grown, but I really miss my dad when he's away.

I started eating. Then I tried again. "I have so much homework for tomorrow, Mamma." (Totally true.) "Maybe I should stay home tonight."

Mamma raised her eyebrows and said, "And when did you get these assignments?"

"Today," I answered, and put a spoonful of beans in my mouth.

"Before or after you went to Mello's?" she asked.

Uh-oh.

I swallowed. "I didn't mean to stay at Mello's so long, Mamma. But you're right. I shouldn't have gone. I have to research a history project, besides math and English."

"We pay a lot for your karate classes, Harmony," Mamma said. I nodded and concentrated on not rolling my eyes. "But it's not just the money. When you commit to something, you need to see it through."

I took a bite of potatoes and wondered if I should explain about my commitment to the Chosen Girls. *That* was a commitment I wanted to see through — all the way through to concerts and money and a new car and house for Mamma. Maybe I could make so much money Papi wouldn't have to travel anymore.

"Harmony?" Mamma asked.

I blinked and focused on her. "Sí, Mamma. You're right," I said. I looked around our house. It's a great house, but it's old. Every room has different colored carpet, and the refrigerator is white but the oven is almond. Stuff like that.

Trin lives in a shiny new house. Sometimes I think it would be nice to live in a house like hers, where everything matches. "Mamma, do you ever wish for a new house?" I asked.

"Sometimes. Usually, I feel blessed to have a comfortable house that's big enough for all of us," she answered. She looked frustrated. "I can see that it will take some work for you to concentrate tonight, so I'm going to let you stay home from karate. But no more going to Mello's until your homework's finished. I don't want you to make this a habit."

If I didn't go to Mello's, we couldn't practice. Without practice, we couldn't get famous. "Fine. I'll go to karate," I said, pushing back from the table.

"No, you won't," Mamma said. "Go upstairs now and start on that history project."

• • •

I got out my folder and history book and hooked my laptop into the router, arranging my stuff around me on my bed. I decided to do one just-for-fun thing before I got started on history. I would keep it quick. I opened a new document and typed in:

Chosen Girls
GRAND OVERALL WINNER
of Channel 34's Music Video Contest
Featured on Channel 34 and Channel 9
Now Available for Concerts!

I thought it looked pretty cool. I played with different fonts. Then I changed the wording. I added:

Now Booking Their Fall Tour

Then I deleted the last line. As long as we were stuck at James Moore, we couldn't have much of a tour. But I started thinking of how many places there are right in Hopetown — community centers, churches, coffee houses. And there are so many towns within an hour's drive, and they have those kinds of places too. I decided I'd better make a list of possible concert sites.

And events! Hopetown has a big Fall Fling every year where bands perform. And there's a holiday lighting at the square and a county fair. So I started listing those too.

It didn't take long to see we could get a really strong start for our band right here, right now. I couldn't help smiling as the possibilities grew, filling screen after screen.

I almost panicked when I realized we only had one song ready. That wouldn't do for real-live concerts. I made a list of songs Mello and I loved to play together. It wouldn't take long to bring Trin up to speed on those.

We'd need more of our own music too. No band that makes it really big does it by playing other people's songs. I made a note to get Mello working on lyrics and Trin working on some tunes. Then I brainstormed some ideas to get them started.

The bedroom door opened, and Julia walked in. She dropped her purse on the desk and started getting her pajamas out of the drawer. "Hey, Harmony. You're hard at work." She glanced at the book beside me. "History?" she asked.

I clicked on "Save As" and typed in "Chosen Girls Ideas." Then I closed the document. "Yeah," I answered. "I've got a project due tomorrow. Why are you home? Did they let you off work early?"

"Early?" she asked. "It's nine thirty. That's when I always get home."

I looked at my digital alarm clock. It read 9:34.

"Oh, no es bueno," I said with a moan. Julia looked at me. "This is taking a lot longer than I expected," I said.

"Well, wrap it up soon," she answered. "I'm ready to go to sleep, and I don't want to do it with the light on and your fingers clicking on the keyboard."

I lifted my laptop off my lap and set it on the bed. Then I got up and stretched. I didn't want to look over my list of assignments for the next day, but I knew I had to.

It was even worse than I thought. I had totally forgotten about the science chart I had to fill out ... on top of everything else. I had to write down what I'd eaten for the last four days and divide it into carbs, proteins, sugars, and stuff.

I sat back down and started in on history. I really focused too. Maybe a few text messages to Mello and a little IMing back and forth with Trin, but not much—for reals.

I didn't do my best work on the project, but I decided it had to be good enough. I felt a knot in my stomach as I saved it to print out in the morning. I reminded myself that plenty of kids do sorry work all the time. Some of them don't even do their homework.

"Please turn off the light," Julia griped.

"Put your head under your pillow," I said. She obeyed but muttered something muffled by her pillow. I didn't really want to know her answer.

I got out my math book. There were three kinds of problems in the assignment I didn't remember ever learning about, so I had to look up the lessons and go back over them. I finished math and got halfway through English before Julia poked her head out from under her pillow and said, "Would you please go work in the kitchen? I can't breathe under here."

I knew if I went to the kitchen Mamma would wonder why I hadn't finished, after staying home from karate and all. Plus, I could hardly keep my eyes open. My day had started before dawn with Doc Wazzup.

I said, "I guess I could stop now and get up early tomorrow."

Julia mumbled, "Por favor!"

I tossed my book and papers onto the floor beside me. I didn't even have the strength to go brush my teeth. I reached for my clock to reset the alarm. I stared at it in a trance. I couldn't think through what work I had left and how much time I would need. I finally set the clock for 5:00, turned off my lamp, and crashed onto my pillow.

Then my brain came alive. I wanted to sleep, but instead, I worried about getting the rest of my assignments finished in the morning. I stressed about Trin being buddies with the Snob Mob. I got upset all over again about Mello's not wanting to do concerts.

I lay there on my back in the dark room, staring at a ceiling I couldn't see. I thought about all the dreams I had for the band.

And I wondered if I could ever make them come true.

chapter • 5

...

I heard something pounding. "*Chicas*, wake up!" Mamma
called through the door.

I couldn't move. It felt like my pajamas were glued to my
sheets. I lay perfectly still.

Julia moaned.

"It's late!" Mamma's voice insisted. "We overslept!"

I opened my eyes and focused on my clock: 7:45 a.m.

"No!" I screamed, flying out of bed. I slipped on the English
papers that covered the floor. "No, no, no! This cannot be
happening!" I yelled as I gathered them up.

"Quit with the drama," Julia said, sitting up and stretching
her arms like she had all day to get ready. "Everyone over-
sleeps sometimes."

"But I didn't finish my work," I cried. "I wanted to get up at
five." I picked up my clock. "Argh. I set it for five p.m."

Julia laughed.

"Your ride will be here in seven minutes," Mamma called.

I stuffed my papers in my backpack and ran to my closet. "Where is my skirt?" I asked, scooting hangers back and forth.

"Which one?" Julia asked.

"My favorite pleated skirt!"

"You have about ten pleated skirts."

"Forget it," I growled. I pulled a pair of cropped pants out of the closet. Totally wrinkled.

"Four minutes," Mamma yelled.

I put them on. I grabbed a T-shirt and pulled it over my head. "I hate this," I said. "I like my clothes to make a statement."

Julia was already tying her shoes. She said, "Oh, those clothes make a statement. They say 'I woke up late.' Or maybe, 'I have no sense of style.' Or—"

I whacked her with a sock, grabbed my boots and backpack, and ran down the stairs. I heard honking from the driveway.

This would be a good time to be a superhero, I thought. *Just step into a phone booth, and wham! You're dressed.*

Mamma stood by the door. She handed me a hot toaster pastry in a napkin and kissed my cheek. "Have a good day," she said. As I ran out I heard her yelling, "Julia, you need to leave in ten minutes!"

I took a bite of pastry as I slid into the backseat next to Mello.

Her mom said, "Good morning, Harmony."

I said, "Good morning, Mrs. McMann," which was a flat-out lie.

I took one more bite, wrapped the rest of the pastry in the napkin, and poked it into my pack. Then I started digging for my science form and a pen. I thought maybe I could get at least some of it done on the way.

Mello said, "Are you feeling okay, Harmony?"

"No, I'm not," I snapped. "I slept late, and I didn't finish my homework, OK?"

Mello said, "Sorry." She sounded hurt, but I didn't have time to worry about it.

We pulled into Trin's driveway, and Mrs. McMann honked. I had three lines filled out by the time Trin got in next to me. I barely glanced at her as I said, "Hey, Trin."

"Hey, Harmony," she said. "Are you trying something new with your hair?"

"Oh, you are so rude!" I said.

"Leave her alone, Trin. She overslept," Mello explained.

"How was I supposed to know?" she asked.

I stretched and tried to see my hair in the rearview mirror. "No es bueno," I moaned, fluffing the sides and smoothing the back. Why hadn't I thought about staying home today? No one would have to see me, and I could finish my work. If only I were famous. Then I wouldn't have to worry about this stuff. No homework. No school. And I'd have people to do my hair and choose my clothes for me.

"Harmony?" Trin asked.

I jumped. "Huh?"

"Were you trying to finish that paper?"

I looked at the science form in my lap. "Oh, yeah," I said. "This is one of four subjects I need to finish during the ten-minute drive."

But I hadn't even finished science when we pulled into the school parking lot.

I slid into my seat in science, praying that somehow Makayla wouldn't notice me.

"Harmony," she practically yelled. "Did you get a haircut? Look, everyone, Harmony has a new hairstyle today. It's very ... sleek." She started laughing. "It almost looks like she didn't wash it."

I just got out my form and tried to finish filling it out. I couldn't remember what I ate for dinner the night before, so I made stuff up. At least I had one subject completed. Anyway, it was all my history teacher's fault.

History!

"Aaargh!" I yelled. Everyone looked at me. Not what I wanted today, of all days. But I couldn't help it. I had stayed up all night to do that dumb history report, and then I had forgotten to print it out! I hid my face in my hands and tried not to cry.

The Chosen Girls needed to do something big, fast. Then maybe Mamma and Papi would be so distracted they wouldn't notice my grades.

After science I ran for the nearest bathroom. Surely I could do something with my hair before I saw —

"Hey, watch out," someone said. I bounced off of whoever I had just plowed into. "Oh, it's you," the voice said.

I looked up, and up even more ... into Cole Baker's aqua blue eyes.

Any other day, running into Cole would be my idea of heaven on earth. But today ... My hair! My clothes!

"Sorry," I mumbled, and took off down the hall.

I got into a bathroom stall before I totally lost it. I had seen Cole a grand total of twice since school started. The first time, I fell up the stairs, and the second time, I had greasy, unbrushed hair and ugly, wrinkled clothes.

I leaned against the stall door and tried to convince myself I could live without Cole. Obviously someone as cool and cute as him didn't need someone as pitiful as me in his future.

Unless … If I got so famous that people everywhere loved me, maybe he would forget. I closed my eyes and pictured it:

We walked through the backstage area of Gibson Amphitheater as our bodyguards led us down a walkway, roped off to hold back the chanting, screaming fans. Ahead, I see our giant bus with Chosen Girls *painted on the side.*

We've almost reached it. Above the roar of the crowd, I hear a voice calling, "Harmony!" I look over the sea of faces … and see Cole.

I give him the cool little "I see you, but I'm acting like I don't see you" wave.

"Harmony, please!" he begs. "I have to talk to you!"

Our biggest body guard—six foot seven, bald, and dressed in black leather—looks at me. "You want me to get rid of this punk?" he asks.

I act like I'm thinking it over. "No, let him through," I finally say. "I'll see what he wants."

The guard motions to Cole, and he leaps over the rope and gets down on one knee in front of me. "Harmony, I know we're young," he begins as I peer into his blue eyes. "I've always loved you. Please tell me that someday, when we're older, you'll consider—"

Brrrrrrring!

Ack! The bell! History was starting. My first time to be tardy.

I ran out of the stall and glanced in the mirror as I ran past. I still hadn't brushed my hair.

• • •

Trin and Mello stood together outside the cafeteria door before lunch. "We went through the snack bar line," Trin told me, holding up snack bags of pretzels, peanuts, and cookies. "Raise your hand if you want to eat outside today."

Mello smiled at me. "The weather is perfect," she said. I could tell she tried not to look at my hair. "And we thought you might need cheering up."

I grinned at them. "That or you're embarrassed to be seen in the cafeteria with me today," I said.

Trin said, "Oh, no, of course it's nothing like that."

Mello giggled. "Definitely not. We like your hair that way, don't we, Trin?"

I laughed and stuck my tongue out at them. But I figured if the two of them actually agreed on something, I didn't want to blow it. "Sí," I said. "Let's picnic."

In the shade under the huge palm, the air actually had a tinge of coolness. We ate happily, without a word.

I chewed my last peanut butter cracker and decided to forget about my grades, my tardy slip, my hair, and my wrinkled clothes. *If only the three of us could always get along like this*, I thought.

Mello leaned back on the bench and looked up at the palm fronds. "Isn't this excellent?"

"Sí," I agreed.

Trin smiled. "I can't believe I live in California! It's way fabulous." She giggled. "Today reminds me of a song." I expected her to hum a tune, or maybe tell us the words. No, not Trin.

She stood up and twirled around in the school yard, her arms flung wide, and sang at the top of her voice, "The hills are alive with the sound of music." She even added the "Ah-ah-ah-ah" before Mello and I managed to grab her and drag her back to the bench.

"What can we do with this loco girl?" I asked.

Mello shook her head. "We definitely won't get bored with her around."

•••

Mello and I said goodbye to Trin and headed to yearbook early.

"I love your suit!" I told Mrs. Gates as soon as I saw her plaid jacket and pleated skirt.

Mrs. Gates just smiled and said, "I've already made the assignments, Harmony."

I felt my face heat up. "Mrs. Gates! I really do like it. I love plaid. And pleated skirts. Ask Mello."

Mello shook her head and said, "In the hall, Harmony told me no matter what you had on, she was going to compliment you so you'd let her be a photographer."

My mouth fell open.

"I'm kidding," Mello added.

Mrs. Gates laughed. "We're just teasing you, Harmony. It's okay."

A few other kids drifted in, and we sat down.

The bell rang, and I congratulated myself for being in my seat on time.

"I'll begin class by announcing your positions on the yearbook staff," Mrs. Gates said. "It is an honor to be part of the crew who puts the James Moore yearbook together.

Remember that no matter what your position is, you have important responsibilities. One of the biggest is to be sure your work reflects well on our school and its students." She looked around the room and smiled. "These books will be treasured for years to come. We want to create a book that each student will feel proud to show his or her children someday."

Wow! It seemed kind of overwhelming when she put it that way.

She started reading assignments. When she said, "Harmony Gomez: photographer," I wanted to scream with happiness.

Mello got layout staff, so we were both happy.

Mrs. Gates gave me my hall pass, a camera, and a speech about what makes good photos (close-ups and action shots). Then she sent me to the second floor to shoot pictures. I felt pretty important walking around while everyone else sat in class. The halls seemed bigger without kids in them, and my boots sounded loud on the stairs. I hoped a teacher would walk by and ask what I was doing in the hall. I practiced flashing my pass.

I wished my hair looked better for all this strutting around and popping in on classes, but I couldn't let that hold me back. I peeked in the open door of the first class I came to. No one looked up. Actually, all the students looked like they were about to fall asleep. I glanced at the teacher, totally absorbed in writing verb tenses across the whiteboard.

I decided to skip it and move on, but then I spotted Makayla next to the wall, three rows back.

Picking her nose!

I mean, she was going for it. She had her book propped up on her desk, hiding her from the students beside her. But not from me.

I bit my lip to keep from laughing out loud. I hoped she wouldn't stop or look up. I had to capture this moment on film.

I got my camera up, turned off the flash, and zoomed in to get a close-up.

Click.

I got it! I walked softly as I moved on down the hall. Then I stopped to admire the shot. *Oh, yeah*! It turned out great. A true action shot.

• • •

Trin and I sat with the other PE students listening to Coach Howland. I tried not to giggle every time I glanced at Makayla's turned-up nose.

"Today you will choose a team of four bowlers," Coach said. "You will practice bowling together from now till next Friday. On that day we won't suit up. Instead, we will load onto buses and go to Barry's Bowling Alley for a tournament."

"Ohwow, how fun!" Trin whispered.

"The team who wins first place will receive two PE passes each," Coach continued. "You can use the passes to skip PE any day you want this semester. Most girls save them for days we're running the mile."

Suddenly I really wanted to be a great bowler.

"Your scores that day will also count as a test grade for this bowling unit," she continued. "I'll give you five minutes to choose your teammates and come sign up."

Of course the Snob Mob went over and signed up immediately. Trin and I found Sidney and Becca, who had always been really nice. I just hoped they were good bowlers, because I really wanted to beat the Snob Mob.

•••

After the last bell rang, I got my books out of my locker and slammed it shut, relieved I'd made it through the day. I walked outside and headed down the steps.

A flurry of white whipped past my head. It took a second to figure out it was papers flying. The wind caught them and carried them onto the green lawn. Others covered the sidewalk. *Oh, no!* I thought. *Somebody's losing all their schoolwork.*

I started to catch one, and then I saw Makayla stomping on and grabbing the papers, sheet by sheet. Too bad I didn't have my camera.

Trin bounded past me on the stairs and ran onto the grass. She gathered up papers, made a neat little stack, walked over to Makayla, and handed it to her with a smile.

I heard Mello's voice behind me. "What did I tell you?" she asked. "Trin does want to be friends with the Snob Mob."

chapter • 6

...

"Let's have some serious jamming, amigas," I said with a smile. Yesterday afternoon Mamma made me stay home, but I'd talked Trin and Mello into meeting at the shed today, just for funsies.

I played a few notes and tuned. *Keep it fun,* I reminded myself.

"Ohwow, it feels like forever since we've been here," Trin said, looking around the shed. "I can't believe Doc Wazzup's interview was just three days ago." She plucked a few notes. "What should we start with?"

"Let's do 'Glitter Jam,'" Mello said, looking at me. I smiled, and so did Trin. Mello tapped four counts to get us started.

We sounded great. "Glitter Jam" is a fun song, with cool parts for all of us. In the middle of it, Trin nodded to Mello, and Mello went off with a serious drum solo. She ended with a cymbal crash and pointed a drumstick at Trin. Trin played some intense guitar riffs and then nodded to me. I felt the music pour through me, into my bass. I thought, *I love this. This is what I was born to do.*

In front of thousands of screaming fans.

Who pay me lots of money.

When the song finally ended, Trin said, "Sweet! We rock."

"Definitely," Mello agreed.

I thought, *This is the time.*

"Hey Mello, have you written any more lyrics?" I asked. I messed around with my guitar, like I didn't really care either way.

Mello tapped a few beats before she said, "I have something you can look at. It's nothing great."

"Cool frijoles!" I said. "Let's see it."

Mello went and got a piece of yellow notepaper. She handed it to Trin.

Trin read aloud:

Love Lessons

Chorus:
Let my love grow.
Let my love show
In every word I say.
Help me reach out
Beyond the doubt
And make this world a better place.
Oh, oh, oh!
Let my love grow.

Bridge:
'Cause with you
I find my soul.

I can't go wrong.
I'm not afraid.
Keep on teaching me, reaching me,
Telling me, helping me to
Be the person I should be.

Chorus 2:
Let my love grow.
Let my love show
In every deed I do.
Help me reach out
Beyond the doubt.
Open my heart
To follow you . . .
Oh, oh, oh!
Let my love grow.

"Sweet," Trin said after she finished. "Mello, this is beautiful."

Mello's face turned hot pink. She said, "Thanks. It came to me when I read Philippians 1:9. It says, 'And this is my prayer: that your love may abound more and more in knowledge and depth of insight.'" She started messing around on her drums again.

I said, "Great. OK, Trin, make up a tune."

"Yeah, right," Trin answered. "It's not that easy, Harmony. I can't just come up with something immediately."

"You did before," I reminded her. "You wrote the melody for "You've Chosen Me" in about five minutes. Have you lost your touch?"

"I heard a tune in my head the first time I read the words for 'You've Chosen Me,'" Trin said. "Don't expect that to happen every time."

I looked at Mello. "Then we need better lyrics," I said. "Mello, did you spend much time on these?"

Mello's eyes got big, and she blinked real fast. "I told you not to expect much," she said.

I rolled my eyes. "I do expect a lot. You are talented—both of you. The first song you guys wrote blew everyone away. I assumed you would get better, not worse."

Trin frowned. "You write a song, then, if you think it's that easy," she challenged.

Argh. "I wish I could," I answered. "But that's not my job. I'm the manager."

Mello looked confused. "What are you doing, Harmony? I thought today was just for fun."

Uh-oh. I tried to cover.

"I think being good at what I do is fun," I said. "And I think jamming to our own music—instead of stale stuff that's been around forever—is fun."

Trin unplugged her guitar. "Well, I don't think this conversation is fun," she said. "I'm out of here."

"Wait, I'm sorry," I said. "We can just play." I tried to smile and calm down. "Even the Beatles—the biggest rock band ever—started by playing other people's stuff. What's your favorite song, Trin?"

Trin looked up at me. I smiled bigger.

"Live to Give," she answered.

"Excellent," Mello said.

I looked at them both. "I don't know it. Will you teach it to me?"

Trin straightened up. "Fine. But no more diva tantrums, Harmony."

"I promise," I said.

Trin started picking notes on her guitar. I liked the sound.

"Just so you guys know," I had to add, "the Beatles played other people's music when they messed around, but they stuck to their own stuff when they recorded and did concerts."

Mello played a driving beat. "Well, since we aren't worried about recordings and concerts," she said, "I guess we can relax. It's not like the Chosen Girls are going to be the next Beatles."

I looked at Trin. She just shrugged and kept playing.

•••

After practice, I headed next door to Lamont's house.

"You again? What's up?" he asked.

I pulled a disk out of my bag. "I want to show you what I've been working on," I explained. "And since you're practically a computer genius, I thought you could help me improve it."

"Practically?" he asked, motioning for me to come in. "What's with *practically*, as in almost? There is no *practically* about it."

I followed him to the media room. "Sorry, Lamont." I handed him the disk, and he put it in a computer. I pulled up the Chosen Girls flyer.

"This isn't bad," he said. "But you were right to come to me."

Lamont added graphics and messed around with the fonts. He read part of it out loud: "Award-Winning Chosen Girls; Now Available for Live Performances."

He looked my way. "I'm afraid to ask how you got Mello and Trin to agree to this," he said.

"Well," I said. "They haven't exactly agreed, yet."

Lamont pushed CTRL+A on the keyboard, and the entire flyer was suddenly highlighted in black. "It will only take one click of the delete button for me to erase this whole thing, Harmony," he said. "Let me save you from yourself." He held his pointer finger just over the DELETE key.

"Don't!" I cried. "I'm not planning to do anything with the flyers now. I just want to be ready. That way, when Trin and Mello give the signal, we won't waste any time."

He didn't move his finger. "You scare me, Harmony," he said.

"Don't be scared, Lamont," I stared at his finger. "Mello and Trin are my best, best friends. I love them. I don't want to make them mad."

He grabbed the mouse and undid the highlighting. The flyer was intact. "I don't know if I should believe you, but I do," he said. "So you guys are getting along better?"

I crossed my arms and leaned back against the counter. "Sí. Better. But Mello and I wonder about the real reason Trin doesn't have time for the band."

"What do you suspect?" Lamont asked.

I leaned toward him and whispered, "Maybe she's decided we aren't good enough. She keeps kissing up to the Snob Mob."

"Kissing up or being nice?" he asked.

"What's the difference?"

"There's a big difference," he said. "And Mello?"

"Same old, same old," I said. "She's not into being in the spotlight like Trin and me. We just don't get her sometimes."

Lamont grinned and pointed at me. "So you're the only one without issues," he said.

I nodded. "Pretty much. Unless you count being stuck between Mello and Trin."

"The monkey in the middle," Lamont said with a sigh.

I tilted my head. "Are you calling me a monkey?" I asked.

He shook his head. "You know. It's a kids' game."

"Oh," I said. "Well, the name fits me. I'm the middle kid in my family, and now I'm in the middle of my two best friends."

"Let me give you a tip," he said. "Be nice and be honest. That's the only way you'll keep their trust. If they don't trust you, the band will break up."

"Thanks, Dr. Lamont. Hey, will you print out one flyer so I can look at it?" I asked.

He did.

"Cool frijoles," I said, looking over the sheet of paper. "Lamont, you are a genius."

"Tell me something I don't know," he replied. Then he added, "I had an idea about the Chosen Girls. For when *all* of you are ready."

"What? Tell me," I said.

"I want to make promotional DVDs of the "You've Chosen Me" video. We could put your contact information on the cover," he said.

I clasped my hands together. "DVDs! Lamont, you're right about yourself. You are beyond genius." I waved the flyer around and headed for the door. "Thanks for your help with this. And start cranking DVDs. Mis amigas will be ready soon!"

That night I had a totally random dream. I sat in Mrs. Burledge's class, and the end-of-class bell rang, but she droned on and on about present perfect participles. I knew I'd be late to PE, and when the teacher finally let us out, I mumbled, "Please, God, let me make it on time."

Next thing I know, I'm bounding down the hall — not flying, exactly, but not just running. I felt like a deer leaping, weaving through the crowds. Kids looked at me and said, "Wow! Who is that?"

I realized I had on my superhero suit—the one from our music video. And I knew, all at once, the superhero thing wasn't just something Lamont did with computer graphics. I *was* a superhero.

Cool frijoles!

I smiled at the mere mortals in the hall as I zoomed past. I made it to PE with time to spare. When Makayla walked in, I realized my powers had to be good for more than getting to class on time.

I opened my backpack. *Oh, yeah.* Sword and shield in place, just like I hoped. I took them out, held up the shield, and waved the sword above my head. I turned to look for Makayla. She stood on a huge stage, singing into a microphone. Trin clapped as Makayla sang, "Harmony is a loser. Everyone knows—"

I aimed my sword at her, waiting for lightning to flash out of it and knock her out. In our video, it took out that demon. Makayla didn't stand a chance.

But nothing happened. Makayla sang away, and I looked down at my sword. Did I have to say something? Was there a button to push? *Crud!* In the music video it just happened.

I got a creepy feeling that someone—or something—was behind me. I turned around. A bone-thin, bright red creature reached long, skinny hands toward my throat. His eyes blazed, and I thought, *He's angry. No, he* is *Anger. He wants to strangle me.* I whipped my sword around and aimed.

That's when I woke up.

chapter • 7

...

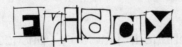

I lay in bed, kinda freaked. I reached up to my throat, half expecting to feel the bony fingers there.

Phew. All good.

Once I figured out I was okay, I remembered the rush of being a superhero. Very cool. A little of that feeling stayed with me the whole time I got ready. Plus, I felt good because I had finished my homework, slept all night, gotten up on time, and taken a shower.

It was easy to take Lamont's advice about being nice. I said, *"Buenos dias!"* as I slid into the McMann mobile. I flashed Mello a huge smile. *"Como estas, mi* amiga?*"*

She smiled back at me. "I'm okay," she said. "Why are you so smiley?"

I patted her shoulder. "Because I'm riding with you," I answered. "What a great way to start my day."

She rolled her eyes.

Trin got in. *"Como estas?"* I asked.

"Fine," she answered. "I take it you're feeling better today?"

I gave one huge nod and said, "Sí! It's a *muy bonita* day, and I'm so happy to be spending it with mis amigas!" I added, "Hey, Mello, I've been thinking about your lyrics. They're amazing. I don't see how you think of that stuff. I sure couldn't.

"And Trin," I continued, "I'm sorry I pushed you about a tune. A brilliant mind like yours needs time to process and create."

I gave them each a shoulder squeeze. "Just relax. Forget what I said yesterday. That kind of pressure won't help you create the songs that will be rocking America for decades to come."

Mello said, "So that's what this is about. It's just your newest way to get us to do what you want."

I tried to look shocked. Actually, it wasn't hard because I was shocked. Shocked that Mello could see through me so well.

"This is not about me," I stammered. "It's about all of us."

"Sure, Harmony," Trin said.

Mrs. McMann parked the car. Trin and Mello bailed out. They were halfway to the building by the time I found my backpack.

• • •

"Today's lesson is on personal hygiene," Mr. Schmidt said. "This is a lesson that can't be overemphasized. Please pay attention for your own good," he held his nose, "and the good of those around you." We laughed, and he let go of his nose. He looked toward the back of the class. "What is it, Makayla?"

"I'm wondering, sir … Are you going to talk about washing hair?"

Mr. Schmidt ran a hand over his blond crew cut. "Yeah. To be honest, washing hair is pretty low on my list of concerns, though. I planned to start with general showering and bathing issues. OK, everybody, open your books to page twenty-seven."

He looked up and said, "What are you talking about back there, Makayla?"

I refused to turn around and look at her, but I couldn't plug my ears. She said, "It's just that I've noticed someone in this class who doesn't seem to know about washing her hair. Like yesterday — it looked so gross! I'm worried about lice."

A few kids said, "Ew!" and "Nasty."

"Fine, Makayla, I'll be sure and cover hair washing and lice. Now please quit talking and turn to page twenty-seven."

Finally the bell rang, and I rushed for the door, but I didn't make it in time. Makayla called, "I'm so glad you were here today, Harmony."

I didn't look back, but she kept talking. In the hall she yelled, "I took some notes for you, Harmony, on how to avoid lice. I'll give them to you in PE."

I gritted my teeth. *If only my sword and shield really were in my backpack …*

Later in yearbook, Mrs. Gates told me to download the pictures I had taken so far. She wanted me to check which ones had potential to make the book and crop them if I needed to.

Mello and the layout staff sat at computers on the other side of the room learning how to arrange photos and text on a page.

I clicked through my pictures of kids doing science experiments in chemistry and stirring ingredients in home economics. Some of the photos were blurry, and a few of them looked too dark, but I saw several that made me proud.

Then I got to Makayla. There she sat in all her glory, her pointer finger shoved halfway up her nose.

I pulled the disk out of the computer and strolled casually over to Mello. "Do you want some photos to work with?" I asked.

"Definitely," she said. "If I can figure out how to import them."

I stuck the disk in. "Let me show you the best ones," I said.

"These look great," Mello said. She smiled at me. "You're a pretty good photographer."

"Gracias," I said, then bit my lip to keep from laughing as Makayla's face filled the screen.

Mello burst out laughing then quickly covered her mouth.

"I think this deserves a full two-page spread," I whispered, tapping the screen.

Mello said, "Harmony! You are evil!"

I shook my head. "No, she is evil," I said, pointing to Makayla's picture. "I am just beyond sick of her!"

"I agree, but we can't humiliate her in the yearbook," Mello insisted. "That doesn't exactly fit in with that Philippians verse about love."

"Would you just make me my own little mock-up?" I asked. "I could keep it in my room to cheer me up. Por favor?"

Mello grinned. "I guess I could do that," she agreed. "Let me see if I can figure it out."

She clicked and double-clicked until the picture showed up in one of the layouts she had already done. It filled the biggest space. "Excellent!" she said. Then she pointed. "We can put a caption here."

"How about, 'Makayla picks a winner,' or 'Makayla digs deep.'"

"You're so mean," Mello said, smiling as she typed.

Later, Mrs. Burledge let us out of English on time for once. Trin and I got to the gym at the same time.

"I don't see why we have to suit up to roll a plastic bowling ball," Trin said, digging in her bag for PE clothes.

"Sí, it's a pain," I agreed. I found my T-shirt in the depths of my bag and tugged on it. A large sheet of paper came out with it and landed at Trin's feet.

"Is this for yearbook?" Trin asked, stooping to pick it up.

I reached for it.

"Wait," Trin said, holding the layout so I couldn't reach it. "I wanna see."

"Isn't that a great shot?" I asked with a giggle.

Trin turned back to me, and her eyes looked big and sad. She folded the paper in half and said, "Harmony, tell me you aren't going to put this in the yearbook."

"Why do you care?" I asked.

"Because that would be a rude, hateful thing to do," she said. She handed it back to me. "I thought you were better than this."

A few people looked at us as they walked past. "Everyone has a breaking point, Trin." I lowered my voice to a whisper.

"I'm crazy-angry with Makayla. Maybe if you weren't so busy trying to kiss up to her like everyone else at this school, you'd be able to see what a twit she is."

Trin whispered back, "Maybe if you weren't so focused on Makayla, you'd realize what a twit you're becoming."

She stomped off to the locker room.

That afternoon I talked Julia into driving me around town. Not that it takes a lot of convincing to get her to drive.

First we went to a print shop where I made color copies of the Chosen Girls flyer Lamont had printed out. I had told him I wouldn't use it right away, but somebody needed to do something to promote the band. And it wasn't technically right away. A whole day had passed since we made it.

Even Julia thought the flyer looked cool. She said, "Very professional. Very snappy." It should be professional and snappy. It took a third of my savings to pay for the copies.

Afterward, we went to the chamber of commerce, two coffee shops, and three rec centers.

At each place, I strutted in, smiled at whoever sat behind the desk or stood behind the counter, and said, "Hello. My name is Harmony Gomez, and I'm the bass guitarist and manager for the hottest new band in Southern California, the Chosen Girls. You've probably seen us on TV."

Even though only one person had heard of us, I left a stack of flyers at each place. I made a little speech about our band and how we wanted to start doing concerts. Each worker said something encouraging. By the time Julia and I drove home, I figured my cell would be ringing itself silly.

• • •

I decided to stay in and do homework. Not much of a Friday night, but I needed to make up for my disasters at the beginning of the week.

Plus, I wanted to be alone to answer those first concert calls. I hadn't quite figured out how to explain my plan to Trin and Mello.

I had dinner with my family and finished two subjects. Still no calls. I stared hard at my cell phone. "Come on, ring," I whispered.

And it did!

I jumped about two feet off my bed. Then I answered in a very professional voice. "Chosen Girls. This is Harmony speaking."

"What in the everglades was that?" Mello asked.

I made myself laugh. "Ha! I'm just messing with you. Hello, Mello." Mello must have been calling from her house phone because it wasn't her ring tone.

"Hey, Harmony," she said. "Did you have fun with Julia?"

I panicked. How did she know what Julia and I had been doing today?

Then I remembered—I had told her and Trin I needed to spend time hanging with my older sister.

"Sí," I answered. "Julia's all right sometimes."

"What did you do?"

"Um ... we went to the Dayton Rec Center. And we messed around." Time to change the subject. "Did you finish your homework?"

"I've still got some English. How about you?"

"Math."

"Hmm. Do you wanna hang out at the shed tomorrow?"

I couldn't stay in forever. "Sí. Sounds bueno," I answered.

Mello said, "Hey Harmony, I don't want to lose Trin's friendship. I don't really think she wants to be in the Snob Mob. I think she's just—"

"Well, I think you were right," I interrupted. "She defends Makayla every chance she gets. She walks the halls with Ella like they're best friends. She's driving me loco."

Mello got quiet. Then she said, "Oh."

I said, "Don't worry about it, though. She'll figure out Makayla Simmons is a loser and we're winners." I looked at the yearbook mock-up and the Chosen Girls flyer side by side on the bed. "She's going to figure it out real soon."

chapter • 8

...

I flipped through a magazine on the couch in the shed. "Do you only love these kneesocks?" I asked, holding the picture out for Trin to see. I had decided to be the mature one and overlook how rude she'd been.

"Cute," Trin agreed.

My phone rang. I grabbed it and said, "Hello?"

A voice said, "Yes, this is Marlo Mansfield. I'm trying to reach Harmony Gomez of the Chosen Girls."

I practically jumped off the couch and walked to the far side of the shed. "This is she," I said. "How can I help you?"

"Actually, this is going to sound a little crazy, Harmony, but I'd like to know if the Chosen Girls could open for the Fall Fling tomorrow."

I looked around. This couldn't be real. Maybe I hadn't woken up.

"Harmony?" she asked.

"Sí. I mean yes, I'm here." I stepped out of the shed and closed the door behind me. "Do you mean *the* Fall Fling? At the Hopetown City Park?"

She laughed and then started explaining. "We generally book our bands up to a year in advance. We've had No Clemency lined up since last August. Then yesterday their manager called and said the band is splitting up. I saw your flyer at the chamber of commerce."

I started to smile. This *was* real. My dream was coming true!

"A couple people on the committee have seen your video, and they love it," she continued. "They thought your band would add a fresh touch to the event and draw in the teen crowd."

I finally kicked into manager mode. "Sí! They're right! The Chosen Girls are exactly what you need!"

"But is the band available on such short notice?" she asked.

"Good point," I said. "Let me look through the calendar of appearances." I reached up and rustled a palm branch for a sound effect.

"It appears to be your lucky day, Marlo Mansfield!" I declared. "The band has tomorrow open."

"Terrific!" she said. I could hear the relief in her voice. "Now, this won't be a full concert. We just need three or four songs to get things rolling. Because of that, we traditionally pay only three hundred dollars."

I wanted to scream, "Cool frijoles!" but I just said, "Three hundred will be fine. What time should we be there?"

"Why don't you set up by three tomorrow afternoon? We'll have a complete sound system there, so don't worry about that. The Fling begins at four."

"The band will be there, Ms. Mansfield. We look forward to doing business with you."

After I hung up, I flung open the door to the shed and yelled, "The Chosen Girls rock Hopetown!" I ran in and grabbed Trin and then Mello in a big hug.

I jumped up and down and clapped and whooped. I danced around in circles. When I stopped, I looked at Trin and Mello.

They sat staring at me.

I realized they didn't know the exciting news. Then I realized they might not consider it exciting.

Oh, well.

"Amigas, that was a lady from the Fall Fling committee." I took a deep breath and let it out. "She wants us to open the Fall Fling tomorrow!"

"What's the Fall Fling?" Trin asked.

"Only the biggest event in Hopetown!" I answered, waving my hands around. "Everyone goes to it. They've got dancers and singers and food booths and crafts, and it's awesome."

"It's excellent," Mello agreed. "You'll love it, Trin. But what do you mean, Harmony, about opening it? Like take tickets at the gates?"

I laughed and hugged myself. "Oh, no, no, no. You are thinking way too small. She wants the Chosen Girls to be the opening *band*. We kick off the whole event!"

Trin's face lit up. "Like a concert?" she asked.

I smiled. I knew Trin would get into it.

"Sí. But just three songs."

Mello held her hands up. "Nope. I told you, Harmony, no live performances."

"Oh, get over it, Mello!" Trin snapped. "This will be a blast."

Mello looked away and started tapping on her legs. I had to act quickly. "Mello, the poor lady practically begged me. She's desperate. They had a band booked for over a year, and the jerks cancelled on them yesterday."

Mello looked at me. She was weakening.

"Think how hard it will be for her to find someone else, with one day's notice," I continued. "And ..." I paused dramatically, "they'll pay us three hundred bucks."

"Get out!" Mello said.

"I'm serious. Three hundred dollars."

"That's a hundred each!" Trin squealed.

"Wow, Trin, you're a math genius," Mello said.

Trin smirked at her.

Mello tilted her face a little and squinted at me. She asked, "Harmony, how did this woman find out about us?"

I gulped. If Mello knew about the flyers, she would bail. "Our video is on TV, Mello," I answered. "She said a couple committee members mentioned it. They love us!"

Whew. I hadn't needed to lie.

"So it's not like we went looking for this, Mello," Trin said. "It fell into our laps."

Well ...

"And we'd be helping someone," I added.

"And we'll get paid for it," Trin said with a hopeful grin. "A hundred dollars for three songs is better money than you'll ever make babysitting!"

I got on my knees in front of Mello and clasped my hands together. "It's just three songs!" I said, blinking my eyes and trying to look pitiful.

Mello looked up at the ceiling. "You make me crazy!" she said. "Both of you." She got up off the couch, and I thought she would stomp out the door.

Instead, she shook her head and grinned. She said, "We'd better practice, don't you think?"

I happily suggested the songs I had listed on my computer a few nights back. Secretly, I thought, *It's a good thing someone in this group has a vision*.

We ran through them, and Trin did okay playing lead and singing. Not great, but okay. I think adding Trin messed Mello up. She didn't sound as good as she usually does.

I knew we had to rock at the Fall Fling. If we blew it, it might be our last appearance.

I gave Mello and Trin some helpful tips.

"Trin, the ending should be soft, not harsh."

"Mello, I can hardly hear your bass drum."

"Trin, we changed keys after the second verse. Didn't you hear us switch to G?"

"Mello, what's with the cymbal crash? It doesn't fit at all."

Once I saw Trin roll her eyes, and Mello did the huffy-puffy after the third song. I tried to stay focused. But Trin said, "Ease up, Harmony. We're doing our best."

"Well," I answered, "we'll never get better by telling each other how great we are," I said. I used a syrupy-sweet voice to say, "That was absolutely delightful. We don't need to improve, because we're already perfect."

"That's not what she meant," Mello said.

"And how do you know what she meant?" I asked. I looked at my watch. "Forget it. We don't have time to fight, amigas. We need three songs by tomorrow. I say we close with "You've Chosen Me," but it would be great to open with our own song too. Trin, have you worked on the tune for Mello's new lyrics?"

Trin gave me a cocky little smirk and said, "Actually, I have. Do you want to hear what I've got?"

"You didn't tell me!" I said in surprise.

"You didn't ask," she answered.

•••

After practice, we headed to Lamont's to share the good news and beg him to help.

He stepped onto the patio, looked at us, and said, "Don't tell me. There is a video contest in three weeks, and you want me to produce an award-winning video for it."

Trin shook her head. "Lamont, that is so last month," she said.

He held up a hand. "Wait. I know. This time you want a full-length feature film."

"Even better!" I blurted. "We're opening for the Fall Fling tomorrow!"

Mello asked, "And we need someone to run sound. You game?"

He raised his eyebrows and made his eyes get huge. "That's it? Run sound?"

We nodded.

"What a reasonable request," he said. "I'd love to do it. And congratulations on the gig!" He looked at me. "How did you swing this?"

I shook my head a tiny bit and hoped he could catch the hint. Someday I wanted the glory I deserved for being a seriously great manager, but not now.

Thankfully, Trin answered. "They called us! A band cancelled, and they wanted us to fill in because they love our video!"

Lamont stuck his nose in the air and stroked his chin. "The mighty Lamont scores again!" he said with a grin.

Mello's dad pulled into their driveway.

We ran over and told him our big news. He climbed out of his car, unfolded his tall body, and hugged Mello.

"I have news too," he said. "A friend of mine from Lewisville is looking for a band. They have a big youth event at Ridgeway Park every year. I told him to contact you, Harmony. Is that all right?"

I nodded. "Sure, Mr. McMann."

We left Lamont behind and practically ran all the way to Java Joint. The owner, Lottie, squealed and bragged on us the whole time she made our drinks.

We finally got settled in our back corner booth. I held up my chocolate mocha freeze and said, "I want to make a toast. To the success of the Chosen Girls."

Mello and Trin giggled, and we clanked our glasses together. Just then the door opened and Cole Baker walked in, with Karson and Hunter following him to the counter.

Mello couldn't see them with her back to the door. I grabbed her hand and squeezed it, whispering, "Cole and Karson are here!"

She grinned and blushed. I know she wanted to turn around, but she didn't.

Hunter looked our way. I tried to act like I hadn't noticed them, but Trin said, "Hello, Hunter."

Hunter grinned and nodded at us. Cole and Karson did the same thing. There must be some kind of rule about cool guys not waving at people.

They got their stuff and sat down, and I pretended to follow Trin and Mello's conversation. I couldn't concentrate on anything except how cute Cole is. I made my drink last, to maximize stare time.

As we left, we passed their booth. "Are you guys going to the Fall Fling tomorrow?" Trin asked.

They looked at each other. I think they were afraid she was asking them out or something. "Probably," Karson finally answered.

"We're opening," I said, trying to sound casual.

Cole's eyes got big. "No!"

We all nodded. I said, "We're on at four."

"Cool," Hunter said.

"We'll try to come," Karson added.

I smiled at Cole one more time before we left. Outside, I turned to Mello and Trin. "OK, amigas, now we don't have a choice," I said. "We have to rock."

chapter • 9

...

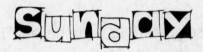

Marlo Mansfield met us behind the Fall Fling main stage, which stood about ten feet off the ground, surrounded by tall palms, a massive banyan tree, and the huge green lawns of Hopetown City Park. She showed us where to plug in and disappeared among the yellow T-shirted people working the festival.

Trin said, "Sweet! California is like some kind of well-groomed jungle." She and I practically skipped up and down the steps as we unloaded and set up. I could already feel my heart pumping.

When Mello finally had her drums situated, she said, "After this, no more concerts. I don't like moving my drums. And I can't believe you talked me into spraying my hair blue again."

"Your hair is blue in the video," Trin said for the millionth time. "It makes sense for it to be blue today. And it looks delicious."

"Whatever," Mello answered. "I'm out-of-my-mind nervous. I want you to pray with me."

I felt a little twinge of guilt. We hadn't been praying enough.

I hadn't been praying enough.

We stepped down and slipped into the shade of a banyan tree behind the stage, taking each others' hands and bowing our heads.

"God, you are so good to us," Trin began. "Thanks for trusting us with this opportunity. I pray that our songs today, and the lives we live, will glorify you."

Mello added, "God, I am so scared. I really do feel weak and afraid, like our song says. Please make me strong."

I prayed, "God, you have chosen us. Help us do our best for you."

We put our hands together in the middle, and Trin and I yelled, "Chosen Girls rock!"

I looked at Mello, expecting her to say it too. She opened her mouth . . . and threw up!

"Oh, Mello," I moaned as Trin and I jumped back. "You can't be sick."

She smiled a weak smile. "Actually, I feel better now," she said.

I ran and got a water bottle and a napkin and handed them to Mello. "At least it didn't happen on stage."

Mello's eyes got huge. I think the thought of throwing up in front of all those people almost made her throw up again.

Trin put an arm around her and led her toward the steps. "I'm glad none of it got on your clothes!" she pointed out.

Marlo appeared again. "It's time!" she said. "Are you ready?"

We got in place, and Marlo introduced us. I couldn't believe how many people had poured in so quickly. The whole park was full.

I've never been more proud of Mello. She turned on a huge smile and yelled, "One, two, three, four," and started pounding her drums like she just lives to do concerts. Trin smiled at her and then me, and I came in on bass. Trin joined on electric, and I thought how incredible this was. *Yesterday this song didn't exist. Today we are playing it on stage in front of hundreds of people.*

It rocked. People started coming toward the stage from all over. They clapped to the beat, and I felt the same electricity I had felt at the award ceremony.

We were halfway through "Glitter Jam" when I spotted Cole and his crew. I flashed him a huge smile, and he smiled back. *Oh yeah*, I thought. *It could happen.*

We closed with "You've Chosen Me." When we got to the second chorus, I thought about the music video Lamont made. I remembered me in my white suit, with a sword and shield, battling the evil monster. I thought about the words to the song and how God makes me strong.

I'd been doing plenty of battling lately, but not so much how God would like me to. Mello was right—we needed to pray … all the time.

After the last song, the crowd cheered, and we left the stage while the next band came up. I felt like I could fly down the stairs.

Lamont stood by the sound booth handing out our DVDs. People shook our hands and said, "Good job" and "You rocked" until my face hurt from smiling.

Trin and I convinced Mello to check out the rest of the fair—even with her blue hair. We ran into Cole, Hunter, and Karson in the arts-and-crafts area.

Cole said, "Great job, Harmony."

I smiled and said, "Thanks, Cole."

My phone rang. I ignored it. It was my generic ring tone. Not important.

Cole said, "Do you need to get that?"

I wanted to say, "I'm looking at the only person I want to talk to." But instead I answered the phone with, "Chosen Girls, this is Harmony speaking."

"Harmony, this is James Smith, from Lewisville," a man's voice said. "I'm looking for a band to perform at the conclusion of Lewisville Youth Week next Saturday. I know that's short notice, but our entertainer fell through."

I covered the mouthpiece and whispered to Cole, "Someone else wants us to perform."

He nodded and looked impressed. Oh, yeah. Cool frijoles. Any minute now he'd be down on one knee.

The man kept talking. "I saw a Chosen Girl flyer at a coffee house, and I just caught your act today. I called my committee members, and they said I should talk to you. Your band is fantastic!"

"Thank you, Mr. Smith," I said. "Tell me about your event."

"It's at an outdoor park a lot like this one. You would play at eleven o'clock in Lewisville."

Something clicked. "Oh, yeah! I've heard about you," I said. "You know Mr. McMann, right?"

At that moment, Cole got down on one knee. For reals! My eyes almost popped out of my face, and I could hardly breathe. Would my crush really propose to me right here, at the Fall Fling?

He started tying his shoe.

" … the mayor of Hopetown." The voice on the phone droned on, while I struggled to concentrate. "Mr. McMann is an old friend."

"He told me you'd need a band," I said. "We'd love to come."

Mr. Smith said, "Great. Let me give you the details … "

I nodded and told Mr. Smith, "OK, I'm ready."

He gave me the park address and his phone number.

I punched it all in my PDA under Contacts and Scheduling. I felt super professional. Until Cole nodded, grinned, and walked off. I want to hang up on Mr. Smith and run after Cole, but I couldn't mess up a whole concert. Not after all my work for the Chosen Girls. *Aargh.*

"I've got your information here on your promotional DVD, so I think we're set. Mr. Smith said, "Do you need directions to the park?"

"No," I assured him. "Mr. McMann knows where it is. He told me all about it."

"Super. We'll see you Saturday at what … ten a.m.?"

"Great," I answered. I hung up and searched for Cole. He was nowhere. "Just great," I repeated.

On the way home, I told Mr. McMann about Mr. Smith's call and our upcoming concert.

"Fantastic. I hope you'll let me take you," he said. "I haven't seen John for a while, and that would give us a chance to catch up."

Mello crossed her arms. "Isn't the band manager supposed to consult the band members before booking concerts?" she asked.

"I didn't need to ask," I explained. "I knew you would say no."

Trin laughed. She said, "Sometimes the manager has to make hard decisions in the best interest of the band."

I thought, *You so do not know how true that is.*

When I got home, I pulled up the calendar on my laptop. Then I pulled out my PDA and looked at the little calendar on it. I clicked on the date I wanted and it said; Concert, Lewisville. I had gotten goosebumps when I typed that in. Then I punched Contacts. The new information didn't show up. I tried every menu option, every button combination. The information for Mr. Smith and the park was nowhere.

What kind of manager loses the information for a concert? I remember typing it in. Crud, I lost my big chance to talk to Cole because of it. But had I saved it? Maybe Cole kinda distracted me ...

How could I admit this to mis amigas? How could I admit it to Mr. Smith? I wanted him to think I was professional.

I felt better when I remembered I had promised to meet him at ten a.m. I put that in my laptop. Then I remembered Mr. McMann knew all about the event. He could tell us how to find the park.

•••

Monday

The next morning Sidney practically attacked me when I walked through the door for science. "Harmony! The Chosen Girls rocked at the Fall Fling! Did you see me? I cheered for you."

I glanced at Makayla. She made a big show of getting her books out and ignoring us, but I knew she was listening. It was exactly the kind of moment I had dreamed about. Time to put her in her place.

"I saw you, Sidney!" I answered. "I'm surprised, because there were *so* many people there. Sometimes when I'm up on stage like that, the crowd just looks like one big mass of yelling, clapping people."

Makayla's head jerked up. "*Sometimes* when you're on stage?" she asked. "You make it sound like you do concerts all the time. Name one other time you were on stage, Harmony." She smiled that tight little smile where the corners of her lips go up, but the rest of her face doesn't participate.

I would not let her win this debate.

"Well, Makayla, channel 34 had this music video contest, and the Chosen Girls won grand overall," I reminded her in a sticky-sweet voice. "I'll never forget being in front of that huge crowd, with everyone rocking to our music. It felt great knowing we were the *best*." I turned back to Sidney. "Our next concert will be Saturday morning, at Ridgeway Park in Lewisville. It looks like I'm going to have to get used to being up front."

Makayla did the huffy-puffy. Then she walked to my desk. In a softer voice than she has ever used to speak to me, she said, "Harmony, you are a joke. Your little band is a joke. I saw you at the Fall Fling, singing about love. You can sing about it, but I don't see you living it." She turned around and went back to her seat.

Of all the rude things Makayla has ever said to me or about me, that one hurt the most. I steamed all through science. I thought, *How dare Makayla Simmons, of all people on earth, lecture me about love.*

•••

At lunch, when Mello left to get more crackers, Trin leaned toward me. "Harmony, you and Mello aren't really going to put that picture of Makayla in the yearbook, are you?" she asked.

My stomach tightened up when I heard that name. I put my forkful of mac and cheese down, because thinking about her made me lose my appetite.

The layout had started as a joke, but it didn't seem funny anymore. It seemed like the only way to get back at Makayla.

"Sí, Trin, we're going to put it in," I answered.

She grabbed my hand. "But Harmony, you're Christians," she began. "Think about the lyrics to Mello's song."

I didn't want to think about the song. I wanted to think about revenge. I stood up and grabbed my tray. "I've already had this lecture today. I don't need it again. Besides, I'm not hungry anymore. Tell Mello I went to the library and I'll meet her at yearbook."

As I neared the yearbook classroom, I heard Mello calling me. I turned around and waited for her.

"What happened at lunch?" she asked. "I went to get crackers, and when I came back, you and Trin were both gone. Thanks a lot!"

"I told Trin to tell you I went to the library. I didn't feel too good." I felt a rush of appreciation for sweet, loyal Mello. "I'm sorry. I didn't know she would leave too."

Mello smiled. "OK. Are you feeling better?"

"Not really." I still had a knot in my stomach. I didn't know if it came from what Makayla said, what Trin said, or what I had decided to do with Makayla's picture. I hadn't ever done anything that mean before.

We walked into class together. Mrs. Gates looked up and said, "Harmony and Mello, I need to see both of you at my desk." She wasn't smiling.

I looked at Mello. She shrugged and looked at me like *What's this about?*

The knot in my stomach felt like it turned into a big, heavy brick when Mrs. Gates said, "Girls, show me the layout you've been working on together. The one featuring Makayla Simmons."

Mello looked like she wanted to kill me.

We walked slowly to Mello's computer and pulled it up. I said, "It's just a joke, Mrs. Gates." She didn't laugh. She deleted the file, and I sighed with relief. Maybe that was all she wanted—to delete it.

"Come back to my desk," she said.

Oh.

I stared at my feet while she talked, because I couldn't stand how sad her eyes looked. She said, "I can't express how disappointed I am in both of you. I chose you for yearbook staff because everything I read in your applications and everything I've seen and heard about both of you made me think you were trustworthy girls.

"You have broken my trust. You have misused your time and the school's equipment. The camera and computer were entrusted to you for the purpose of creating beautiful memories. Instead, you have used them to humiliate and hurt someone."

I didn't think it would matter if I explained how mean Makayla has always been to us, so I just kept quiet.

She went on. "Harmony, I need you to turn in your hall pass for two weeks." I looked up, shocked. "Mello, you will be on probation," she said, "which means I will check your work each day."

Mello nodded.

Mrs. Gates finished up by saying, "Please use this time to convince me I made the right choice by allowing you on staff. At the end of the two weeks, if I am not convinced, you will be transferred to another class during this period."

• • •

As soon as I found Trin in the locker room, I let her have it. "You jerk!" I began. I had a hard time keeping my voice soft, but I tried. I didn't want Makayla and company to hear me. "I wish you never moved here, Trin. Why did you pretend to be friends with Mello and me when all you ever wanted was to be in the Snob Mob?"

She stopped tying her shoe and said, "What? The Snob Mob?"

"Whatever," I blurted out. "Don't act all innocent. You were fine until school started. I've tried to ignore what you've been doing since then, but I've had enough. All you've done is defend them and kiss up to Makayla and Ella."

Trin shook her head. "I don't defend them, Harmony. I just try to understand where they're coming from. And how have I kissed up to them?"

I pointed at her. "I saw you running around to save Makayla's papers that day."

"Please, Harmony, that's not kissing up. That's just helping someone who needs help."

"What about all your chats with Ella after PE?" I accused.

"She's in my ballet studio," Trin explained. "I asked her about how Miss Towns runs rehearsals and recitals. That's all."

I had saved the biggest thing for last. "Well, what about turning me in for the yearbook layout?"

I waited, hoping she would deny it.

She didn't.

"I didn't talk to Mrs. Gates because I want to be in the Snob Mob," she said. "I talked to her because that layout was wrong. No matter how mean Makayla is, it doesn't make it okay for *you* to act like a jerk. She may not know better, but you do. Think about Philippians 1:9. 'I pray that your love may abound more and more in knowledge and depth of insight.' Have you tried to learn about Makayla? Do you have any insight into why she acts the way she does?"

I looked away. "I don't care why she acts the way she does. I just know she doesn't deserve my love," I answered.

Trin grabbed my face and turned it back toward her. She looked into my eyes and said, "The Bible says if we only love people who love us, we're no better than the evil people around us."

I picked up my clothes. "I'm going to change somewhere else," I said. "And forget practicing tonight. I don't want to show up and get preached at. I've had more than I can stand today."

I blinked to keep from crying as I changed into my T-shirt and shorts.

All my dreams for the band were finally coming true.

It didn't seem fair that at the same time the rest of my life was falling apart.

chapter • 10

...

The next day Trin said if we didn't start practicing, the concert was off. So that afternoon I stomped into the shed.

I played around on my bass, warming up, trying to focus on music and ignore Trin. It wouldn't be easy to get through this practice, but I knew I had to. The Chosen Girls had a full-fledged concert in four days, and we only had three songs ready.

I wondered if other bands ever got up on stage and smiled and sang together, then left the stage and ripped each other apart.

Probably.

"We know we can do 'Love Lessons,' 'Glitter Jam,' and 'You've Chosen Me,'" Trin said. "How about 'Stars Above'?"

"Definitely!" Mello said. That's her favorite song.

She started us off, and I came in on bass. It sounded cool until Trin came in. She sounded funny.

I stopped playing. Trin and Mello stopped too and looked at me.

"What?" Trin asked.

"Do you have a cold, Trin?" I asked.

"No. Why?"

"Your voice sounds different. Like you have a stopped-up nose."

"Thanks for the put-down," Trin said.

I said, "It's not a put-down. I'm trying to help the band."

"By telling me I can't sing."

I shook my head. "By telling you not to sing through your nose."

Mello started playing again. She said, "Harmony, be quiet. Trin, ignore her. We don't have time for this."

Trin looked up at the ceiling and started playing again.

I had already been irritated at Trin. Now I felt mad at Mello too. Why practice if we weren't going to try to get better?

I joined in the song, but my heart wasn't in it.

After we finished, someone knocked on the door.

Mello called, "Come in."

Lamont walked in. "Hey, what's up?" he said. "Getting ready for the big gig, huh? You probably need ... what? Ten songs? And you've got four days?"

Trin said, "Thanks, Lamont, but we don't need you to add any pressure. Harmony's doing a good job of that on her own."

"So you're finding out how it feels," he said. "I remember not so long ago when you three came and told me I had three weeks to produce an award-winning video."

"And you did it," Mello pointed out.

"Of course," he answered, throwing his bony shoulders back. "And you'll do it too. I have no doubt the Chosen

Girls will rock, if you remember what worked last time." He stopped talking and looked around. He rubbed his hands together. "It feels kind of weird to be in here without a camera," he finally said.

We laughed.

I said, "I bet. We practically had to surgically remove the thing from your face in time for the awards show."

"Why don't you stay for a while?" Mello asked. "Maybe you can give us some ideas."

"OK, if you think I can help," Lamont said, flopping onto the couch.

During the next song, I watched Lamont. His feet started tapping, and then his arms started moving. Then he stood up and started dancing. I had never seen him dance before, and I could totally see why. He dances even worse than he plays the drums. His long, skinny arms poked out at crazy angles and he pushed his bony shoulders forward and backward. The whole time he swung his legs around like he was riding a bicycle and doing jumping jacks at the same time.

Mello and Trin and I started laughing so hard we couldn't play anymore.

Lamont kept dancing, even without the music. He looked at us with puppy-dog eyes. "You laugh at Lamont, the dancing machine?"

Mello covered her mouth. Then she uncovered it and said, "Lamont, I think your dancing machine is out of order."

"Oh, come on," he insisted. "I've been practicing every day. I know you don't want me recording you anymore."

"Definitely," Mello agreed.

"So I thought I could travel with the Chosen Girls and be your official fly guy. You need a dancer."

I laughed so hard, I felt like I might throw up.

"I tell you what, Lamont," Trin finally said. "You stick with us. Maybe we'll even offer you a contract."

His eyes sparkled. "Oh, happy day!"

She smiled at Mello and me. "Don't you think we should, Harmony?" She asked. "We could offer him twenty dollars per concert."

"Hey, that's not bad!" Lamont said.

I agreed. "No, it's not bad. We'll pay you twenty per show NOT to dance. I'd rather see Mello's dad try to bust a move."

As we packed up after practice, Lamont said, "I could run sound again if you want me to."

We looked at each other. I hadn't even thought about sound. "Great, Lamont! Please do. And, crud. I bet we'll have to bring our own sound system."

"We don't have a sound system," Trin pointed out.

"Let me work on that," Lamont said. "We can probably rent one."

• • •

Wednesday

Wednesday stunk. First, I got back that science chart about everything I'd eaten. Mr. Schmidt took off ten points for sloppiness and another twenty-five points for not break- ing it down into carbs, proteins, sugars, and fats. In red, at the top of the paper, it said *65*. Ouch.

In history we got our projects back. Mrs. Darby counted off twenty-five percent for being a day late—just one day! And she didn't like anything I wrote about. I read over my answers, and to be honest, I didn't like them either. I'd never gotten a *59* before. On anything. Ever.

And it got worse. I don't even want to think about the grade I got back on that English paper I didn't finish. But it slapped me into reality.

This year has just started, I thought. *The teachers will label me an idiot. No matter what kind of work I do from now on, they'll give me low scores.*

What if I never graduate? My only hope is to go on the road with the Chosen Girls. People don't ask rock stars how they did in history or math or even what they ate for an entire week.

Now, more than ever, Saturday's concert had to be a success.

•••

That afternoon we had a hard time getting "Glitter Jam" to sound right. It made me nervous, because it is a pretty easy song—one of the three we thought we had down.

As we started over for the third time, I think we all felt the pressure of the concert hanging over us. My sorry grades didn't help my mood any either.

Mello said, "We can't do this. We'll get in front of all those people and make fools of ourselves. We just aren't ready to do a whole concert."

"It's a little late now, Mello," I said. "We would be ready if you and Trin had done what I said to do." I knew I should stop there, but I couldn't make myself.

"I've been trying to get you to have a serious practice since the day after Doc Wazzup. But no, you wanted to read magazines. You wanted to jam just for fun. Trin had to go to ballet and study. Trin couldn't make the Chosen Girls a priority. No one but me is willing to put in the work it takes to get this band where it needs to be. I've practically quit karate, and I'm failing my classes, all so this band can be a success."

"I'm skipping ballet right now," Trin said. "And I'm not studying for my history test tomorrow. I am making the Chosen Girls a priority, but I won't do what you're doing. I won't obsess about it."

I looked at Mello, ready for her attack. But she didn't say anything. She just sat there looking sad.

Part of me wished she would gripe me out, so I could attack her back. I feel seriously defenseless against that pout of hers.

•••

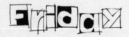

By Friday I forgave Trin for preaching at me, getting me in trouble with Mrs. Gates, and doing the huffy-puffy during every practice.

We had a blast riding the bus to Barry's Bowling Alley during PE. I was way ready for a fun-o-rama time away from school.

Inside the bowling alley, we traded our shoes for bowling shoes. Then we chose our lane and started looking for balls.

"Look! I found a way fabulous pink one!" Trin yelled.

She lifted it off the special shelf and bent almost to the ground. "Ohwow, it weighs like two hundred pounds. I so cannot carry it."

"Then you so can't bowl with it, Goob," I said. "You need a nine or ten, I bet."

She looked at hers. "This is a twenty. But it's pink!" She pouted.

I looked at all the balls, rolling them over so I could see the numbers. "Here's one, Trin," I called. "A pink ten. And a purple one for me!"

We got set up with Sidney and Becca. Makayla and her crew, for once, didn't pick the lane right next to us. They chose two lanes over. What a relief! I didn't want Trin evaluating how loving I acted toward them during the tournament. I had enough to think about.

Sidney started putting our names in the computer. Coach Howland had already explained that it would keep score automatically. I reminded my teammates, "Amigas, it would be seriously great to win those PE passes. And I can't get another bad grade. So let's rock!"

I bowled first. I knocked down six pins on my first roll.

Trin yelled, "Ohwow, Harmony! Go, girl!"

I gave her a high five while I waited for my purple ball to come out of the ball return. Then I focused on the leftover pins, held my ball in the perfect position, and bowled. But my thumb stuck in the thumb hole, and the ball swung up with my arm. When the ball did come loose, it went into the air and then crashed down onto the lane and bounced twice before it landed in the gutter.

Even from two lanes away, I heard Makayla say, "I didn't know bowling balls could bounce!"

I thought of Trin and kept my mouth shut. But I started watching the Snob Mob from the corner of my eye. They didn't have a clue how to bowl. They guttered it more often than they got the ball to the pins. But they laughed and cheered and gave each other high fives like they were winning a TV tournament. I didn't get it.

On Trin's first turn, she got a split. That's where only two pins are left standing and one's on the far left and one's on the far right. On her second roll, she knocked down the one on the right.

Sidney and Becca did great. I decided we had chosen the best bowlers in school for teammates. It looked like we would win, if I didn't get the ball stuck to me anymore.

After a few frames, Trin left to go to the bathroom. When she came back, she said, "Makayla and them have way fabulous scores."

"No way," I answered. "They've knocked down maybe four pins so far."

Trin nodded. "OK. That's what I thought."

She sat in one of the blue molded plastic chairs facing Makayla's lane. She watched them until her turn to bowl. After she bowled, she said, "I'm going to trade for another ball."

She put her pink ball on one of the shelves of balls right behind the Snob Mob. She watched Ella bowl (a gutter the first time, three pins down the second time) and looked at the scores. Then, instead of choosing a new ball, she walked over to Coach Howland.

She came back and picked up her ball. She got to us just in time for her turn. "I couldn't find one I liked better," she said. She walked up and bowled a strike.

Sidney, Becca, and I went crazy.

A few turns later I noticed Coach Howland. She stood at the snack bar, but her eyes were on the Snob Mob. After a few frames, she walked up to them. I couldn't hear what she said, but I heard Makayla's answer.

"We haven't been paying attention to the scores. You mean our scores don't match what we're bowling? Weird."

Coach Howland said something to Bailey. Bailey said, "No, Coach, I wasn't changing our scores."

Coach said something else. Then Bailey said, "Yeah, well, I mean, I thought the computer messed up on that last one, so I tried to fix it."

I had to bowl next, so I couldn't watch them anymore.

After my turn, I whispered to Trin, "You turned them in for cheating, didn't you? But I thought Ella is your big-time ballet buddy."

Trin rolled her eyes. "I don't know how to make you believe me. I don't want to be in the Snob Mob."

"So you turned them in to prove that you like me better?" I asked. Maybe Trin was finally coming around.

Trin's mouth and eyes got big and round. She said, "You don't know me at all, Harmony, do you?"

I shook my head. "No, Trin," I answered. "I don't think I do."

"Right is right, and wrong is wrong, no matter who does it," she said. "That's one thing you might as well learn about me right now. I will always take a stand for what I believe in."

I hoped Trin felt as confident as she sounded, because it looked like the Snob Mob knew who turned them in. The girls were sending some pretty nasty looks her way.

chapter • 11

...

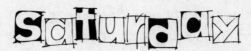

Saturday morning I woke up before my alarm rang.

My eyes popped wide open as soon as it hit me—concert day! Today I would prove myself as band manager, and the Chosen Girls would prove themselves as a band.

I wanted to dance around the room and sing about all my dreams coming true, but I knew from experience Julia wouldn't appreciate it. She didn't have to be at work until 8:00.

Instead of singing and dancing, I jumped out of bed and grabbed my cell. I called Mello as I half-jogged down the hall to the bathroom.

She answered on the third ring. "Harmony, it's six thirty. In the morning. And it's Saturday."

Mello has never been into mornings.

"But today is the day!" I reminded her. "Today the Chosen Girls rock Ridgeway Park!"

She moaned. "Why did you have to bring that up?"

"It's a happy thing, Mello. Just get out of bed and start turning your hair blue," I demanded.

I hung up and called Trin. She sounded sleepy too. "Hello?"

"Trin! It's concert day!"

"Ohwow. What time is it?"

"Six thirty."

"Six thirty? And I'm still in bed! Harmony, you're a life-saver. I'm getting up right now. See you at eight."

I had chosen eight o'clock as our time to leave. I knew a big part of my job as manager would be to get the band to the park on time. I figured leaving at eight gave us time to deal with traffic, unload, set up, and hopefully run through at least a couple songs before we had to meet Mr. Smith.

I grinned as I started the water for my shower. Mr. Smith would be impressed.

• • •

My hair would not work with me. The parts I wanted to stick out stuck flat to my head, and the parts I wanted to lie down poked out. I tried one more time when my phone interrupted me.

I looked at the bathroom clock: 7:30.

I answered, "Hello, Mello!"

Mello said, "Harmony, we have a problem."

I thought my heart might stop. We didn't need problems today. I took a breath and reminded myself this was part of my job as band manager. "What?" I asked. "What is it?"

"Some huge city thing has come up, and my dad can't drive us," Mello explained. "And my mom already had a big librarians' meeting, so she can't take us either. But dad said he can draw a map for your mom or Trin's mom. Are you mad?"

"That's all? No, I'm not mad," I answered. "I'll talk to Mamma. Don't worry about it." *Then Mamma will watch us*, I thought. My Papi, of course, was out of town.

"Thank goodness," Mello said. "I thought you'd be all hissy."

"Me?" I asked, surprised. I don't know why she thought I'd be upset. I don't let stuff like that bother me.

I gave up on my hair and went to find Mamma. She said she'd be happy to drive, but of course she'd also have to bring Richie and MaraCruz. With the Chosen Girls, that meant six in the van. Lamont made seven. She didn't know if that would leave enough room for the equipment.

I called Trin, who asked her mom to drive too. Her mom said sure, as long as she could follow my mamma.

I went to my closet and started digging for my platform high-tops. I only found one. That is seriously frustrating, because when I can't find them at all, it means I took them off somewhere weird and I'll find them by the couch or maybe by the front door. But when I find one, it means one is just flat-out lost.

I had to wear them for the concert. I looked under my bed (seriously scary) and even under Julia's bed. I decided I needed to be more organized if I planned to manage the Chosen Girls.

I finally found the second shoe under my desk, with a T-shirt thrown over it.

As I laced them up, I wondered if having moms and little brothers and sisters in the audience might drastically reduce our cool factor. Then I thought, *There will be so many people there, no one will have a clue they're related to us.*

Mamma got the little ones up and started cooking a big breakfast. I explained that we didn't have time for all that, but she said she didn't want to get there and have everyone complain about being hungry.

I paced around, trying to make it clear what a hurry we were in.

Mamma said, "If you want to speed things up, set the table and help MaraCruz get dressed."

I thought, *Isn't this typical? It's the day of my concert, and I have to help with chores around the house. I hope it won't be long until I can hire a maid and a cook.*

Julia came into the kitchen and grabbed a plate. "Can I take the van to work, Mamma, or will you need it?" she asked.

"I'll need it," Mamma answered. "I'm going to be driving Harmony to her concert."

I stopped pacing and looked at the digital clock on the microwave: 7:50.

"You don't have time for breakfast, Julia!" I said, walking over and grabbing her plate. "Go! Hurry, Mamma, take her!"

Mamma slapped softly at my hand. She said, "Eat your breakfast, Julia. It only takes a couple minutes to get to your store. And you eat too, Harmony. You can't sing on an empty stomach."

"But we're supposed to leave at eight, Mamma!" I cried. "We still have to load."

Mamma just smiled and said, "Mi hija, we'll be fine."

• • •

We finally got to Mello's at 8:15. Mello and her dad came out as soon as we pulled up.

Her dad went over directions with Mamma while Mello and I loaded drums. After our second trip, I thought how great it is that my instrument fits in one portable case.

After we had the drums and amps in, we knocked on Lamont's door.

"Oh, happy day!" he said when he opened the door. "This is big, women. Today could make or break the Chosen Girls."

Mello said, "Please, Lamont, I already feel sick."

Lamont smiled at her. "You'll be fine. Your band rocks. There's only one improvement I would dare suggest."

"What's that?" I asked.

"Put me in on drums," he answered.

Mello and I cracked up.

We helped him bring the sound equipment out to the driveway, but we couldn't fit another thing in the van. The sound stuff would have to go in Trin's SUV, and Trin still wasn't there. I called her cell.

"Ohwow, Harmony, I know I'm late. I am so sorry. We'll be there. It's my hair—it's way ugly today, and I so don't want to go on stage like this!"

Arrgh. I said, "You won't have to if you don't come now, Trin, because we'll miss the whole concert."

"OK. Just let me try one more thing and I'll be there."

I paced back and forth on the driveway, because I couldn't stand still. And I went over the order of songs with Mello.

And I worried.

The SUV finally pulled in. Trin's mom drove so fast I thought she might run over the sound equipment, but she stopped in time.

We loaded everything into the back of the SUV and sent Trin's little brother to ride in my van with MaraCruz and Richie. Then Lamont, Mello, Trin, and I hopped in Trin's car. I flipped open my cell and checked the time: 8:43.

It didn't really surprise me that the highway between Hopetown and Lewisville had a major construction project going on. That just seemed like a given on a day that started the way this one had.

We crawled along at twenty miles per hour. My stomach felt like one seriously wadded-up ball of nerves. I checked the time every few minutes and pulled on my ear until it hurt.

If we didn't get there soon, I would be the one throwing up this time instead of Mello.

I decided I'd better call Mr. Smith so he wouldn't panic.

He answered right away. "Hello?"

"Mr. Smith, this is Harmony. I just wanted to let you know the Chosen Girls are on the way. We've run into some construction, but we'll be there soon."

"OK, Harmony," he answered. "Thanks for letting me know. I've run into a delay myself. If for some reason I'm not there to meet you, just go ahead and set up in the gazebo. I'll be there in time to introduce you."

Finally, we saw a sign that said Ridgeway Park. We followed Mamma's van into the parking lot.

I looked at my phone. It said 10:39.

"Amigas, we have no time to lose," I said, before the SUV even came to a complete stop. "We have twenty minutes until the concert begins."

I saw the gazebo Mr. Smith had told me about. I pointed to it and said, "That's where we're setting up. Start hauling."

"Isn't there a closer parking spot?" Mello complained. "It will take us thirty minutes to walk that far."

"We only have twenty, so I guess we'll have to run," I snapped.

I tucked my phone under the seat of the SUV so I could carry stuff with both hands, and we got busy.

Mr. Smith still hadn't come by the time we had everything in place. I looked around the park. A mom pushed a toddler in a stroller, three skaters rollerbladed on the sidewalk, and some kids played sand volleyball. It looked like a normal Saturday.

What had happened to the dramatic finish to Youth Week?

Trin asked, "Where is Mr. Smith?"

I shrugged. "He said he had run into a delay, but he would be here to introduce us. I guess he's running later than he expected."

Mello looked around. "It doesn't look like anyone is here for the concert."

I refused to let our debut flop. "It must be like the Fall Fling," I said. "They'll come over when we start playing."

Lamont walked up to the base of the gazebo. "So are you going to wait for Mr. Smith, or go ahead?"

They all looked at me. I tried to think like a band manager. What would be the professional thing to do?

"Let's go ahead," I answered. "Trin can introduce us."

I noticed a car parking and hoped it might be Mr. Smith. Some teenagers climbed out and started walking toward us. Finally — someone had come for Youth Week.

Trin grabbed the mike and said, "Hey, Lewisville! Are you ready to rock?" Then she counted us off, and we started our first song.

It was pretty tough to jam with two moms, two six year olds, and a three year old the main part of our audience. I wanted to leave the stage and cry. This concert was not at all what I had pictured.

But I forced myself to play the music. Surely more people would join the fans from that car and head our way.

I smiled in their direction, and then I froze. I seriously stopped playing.

The people from the car—the only teenagers coming to our stinking disaster of a concert—were Makayla and the Snob Mob.

...

chapter 12

Still Saturday

Even though I couldn't hear them over the music, I could see them laughing. Makayla looked right at me and waved her arms around the park. She held her hands up and made a face that said, *This is your big concert?* just as clearly as if she had yelled it into the microphone.

Mello saw them and shot me a desperate look. She missed a beat on the drums, and her voice cracked.

That left Trin pretty much singing alone and playing a solo on her guitar.

I joined back in the song, determined to do my best. So maybe no one showed up. So the Snob Mob was laughing at us. So what? Mr. Smith had hired the Chosen Girls, and we were on stage.

Some volleyball players wandered over before the song ended. Their clapping almost drowned out the Snob Mob's rude comments.

By the end of the second song, a couple moms brought their toddlers over.

By the end of the fourth song, no one else had come, not even Mr. Smith. I desperately wanted to wrap it up, but Trin just kept introducing songs and singing away with all her heart. She followed the plan we had agreed on and never acknowledged that this wasn't exactly what we had dreamed of for the concert.

We finally closed with "You've Chosen Me." Makayla and her crew sang along at the top of their lungs, but of course they sang the bowling version. They even did their little actions. Other people in the very small crowd gave them some serious looks, but it didn't slow them down a bit.

When the song ended, I couldn't even hear my mamma clapping. All I could hear was Makayla's snotty laugh.

"So where's Mr. Smith?" Mello hissed.

"And where are all the people that were supposed to come for Youth Week?" Trin asked.

We were still on the gazebo, and I didn't want to make a big scene. I tried to be cool. "I don't know. Start tearing down, and I'll go check my cell phone. Maybe Mr. Smith called." I thought checking my phone might be a good reason to get away from Mello and Trin before they went into full-fledge attack mode.

"I can't believe I skipped ballet and bombed a history test for this," Trin said, slamming her guitar into the case.

"I told you we weren't ready to do a concert, Harmony," Mello said as she picked up her stool. Tears started rolling down her cheeks. "I knew it would be a disaster. We looked like idiots. This is so totally my worst nightmare, except it's real."

I took my bass and an amp and marched down the stairs without glancing at Makayla. I ignored her comments, grabbed the keys from Mrs. Adams, and practically ran to the SUV.

I threw my case in the back and then fished my phone out from under the seat. I flipped it open.

Four missed messages.

I started listening to them.

Message one: "Harmony, this is Mr. Smith. I guess you're still stuck in traffic."

Message two: "Are you lost? Please call me if you're having trouble locating the park. We've got a great crowd here, ready for the concert."

Message three: "I'm not sure why you aren't answering, Harmony. I've made announcements and stalled about as long as I can. There are over a hundred people here, waiting. I'll try to hold off a little longer."

Message four: "It's eleven thirty. I'm going to have to send the crowd home. I hope you girls are okay. Please let me know what happened, so I'll have something to tell my committee."

I stared at my phone and gulped. This didn't make sense. Mr. Smith must have gone to the wrong park. Mr. Smith and all those people . . .

Because we couldn't be at the wrong park. We had the map Mr. McMann had drawn.

Of course, Mr. McMann hadn't talked to Mr. Smith. I had talked to Mr. Smith. And I had talked to Mr. McMann.

There had to be two Mr. Smiths. And I had booked with the wrong one!

I saw Trin and Mello heading my way. They didn't look happy, and it was about to get worse. I would have to tell them the truth about today's mix-up.

"Harmony, we need to talk," Trin began. She put down her guitar and held a piece of paper out to me. "This was in Lamont's box of DVDs."

I took it. It was a Chosen Girls flyer.

"So?" I asked.

"So?" Mello repeated. "Did you post flyers about our band? Is that really how we got the Fall Fling gig?"

"They really did like our video, like I said," I answered.

Mello put her stool down, sat on it, and crossed her arms. Trin tilted her head and squinted her eyes at me.

I threw my hands up in surrender. "Okay, okay, and maybe they saw a flyer lying around," I admitted.

Trin poked her finger at me. "You lied to us!" she yelled. "I told you I couldn't do anything this semester, and you went around passing out flyers saying we're ready for concerts!"

Mello shook her head. "You tricked me. You knew I didn't want to do concerts, Harmony. But you wanted to be famous, and it didn't matter to you what Trin or I wanted."

I blinked, trying not to cry. "I figured once we did a couple concerts and we were a huge success, you guys would thank me," I explained.

They both rolled their eyes. Trin pointed to the gazebo. "Is that what you consider a huge success?" she asked.

I took a deep breath. "Well, I messed up," I began. "Apparently we did our concert at the wrong park."

"The wrong park?" Mello echoed. "How?"

"I'm not totally sure, but Mr. Smith left a few messages on my phone. He said he just sent the crowd home. There were over a hundred people there ... " I couldn't talk anymore, because I started crying. I didn't know what hurt worse—the thought of all those fans waiting for a band that never showed up, or the pitiful concert we'd just done in front of the Snob Mob, or my two best friends attacking me.

No, the worst thing was knowing I deserved this, and more.

When I could talk again, I said, "I didn't mean to ruin everything. All I wanted was for everyone to be happy." I covered my eyes with my hands and wiped away the tears. I blinked and looked at Trin and Mello. "I really do love both of you."

Trin didn't back down. "That's a nice thought, Harmony. But if you love us, show it."

Mello added, "If you want us to be a band—or even friends—try acting like it. Think about us too. Not just you. That's part of that knowledge and insight stuff we've been singing about."

I nodded and wiped my running nose on the sleeve of my shirt. I felt a weak grin forming and asked, "Maybe the next song we sing could be about forgiveness?"

Mello giggled. She threw her arms open and said, "I forgive you, Harmony."

I started crying again as I hugged her.

"Me too," Trin said. She joined our hug.

I heard Lamont's voice say, "Me too. Whatever we're talking about. Do I get to join the hug?"

Trin said, "Go away, Lamont."

"I will after you pay me," he answered.

We pulled away from our hug, and I said, "What are you talking about?"

He shook his head. "How quickly they forget," he said. "You owe me twenty bucks—for not dancing."

•••
Saturday Night

Two weeks later, Trin and Mello and I fought over the mirror in the tiny bathroom before we went on stage.

"So the first Mr. Smith told all the people from the Youth Week concert we missed to come tonight too?" Mello asked.

"Yeah," I answered. "So nice. And the second Mr. Smith was seriously cool to go ahead and book us for this event — the one he'd told Mr. McMann about — even after I totally messed up the Youth Week concert."

"Ohwow, they're both way fabulous to give us another chance," Trin said as she brushed powder over her nose. "And now we get to perform for a crowd that's twice as big. I'm proud of you for asking them, Harmony."

"I didn't want to," I admitted. "I really wanted to move to Greenland. I was totally embarrassed when I figured out Mr. McMann and I had been talking about two different Mr. Smiths and two different shows all along."

"My dad feels bad too, Harmony," Mello said. She patted my shoulder. "But everyone makes mistakes."

Someone pounded on the door, and Trin screeched, "No! I'm not ready. It can't be time!"

I opened the door and saw Papi! I ran into his arms.

"Harmony!" he said, squeezing me till I could barely breathe. "I just got into town. Your mamma told me to come straight here."

I heard my older brother say, "Me too. Mamma said it would be a good weekend to come home from college."

MaraCruz squeezed in and hugged my leg. She squealed, "Me too, me too!"

I reached out for Richie, who stood back watching. He came and hugged me on the other side. Next thing I knew Julia and Mamma joined in. There I was, smashed in the middle of my whole familia.

In the middle — like always — and it felt great.

When I could break away from them, I went back in to finish getting ready. I looked at my best friends' faces, reflected on either side of mine in the mirror. "You know, not everyone has friends like you two who forgive them for acting like a selfish brat. And who agree to do another concert even when they don't have time." I looked at Trin. "Or don't like doing them." I finished, looking at Mello.

They both smiled back at me, and once again I felt like being in the middle wasn't so bad after all.

"Maybe I could make Philippians 1:9 my life verse," I said. "I have a lot to learn about love, that's for sure."

Trin threw one arm around my shoulders and said, "We all do." She fluffed her hair. "You know, at first I was bummed out when they moved this event to a gym, but now I'm so psyched. I love our idea." She stopped, and her eyes got huge. "Wait a minute. Are you sure we're at the right gym, Harmony?"

I actually caught my breath. Then I let it out and elbowed her. "We've rehearsed here twice, Goober," I reminded her. "And it wasn't *our* idea — it was *your* idea. The best idea ever!"

She hugged herself. "It *is* a good idea," she agreed. "But we couldn't do it without your fashion design skills."

"And Mello's sewing skills," I added.

Mello giggled. "I hate to admit it," she said. "But we definitely couldn't do it without Lamont." She messed with the ribbons on her shirt. "Know what? I'm actually psyched about tonight too. Do you think it will really work?"

I shivered with excitement. "I hope so."

We held hands and prayed in the small bathroom.

"Thanks, God, for giving me better friends than I deserve," I prayed. "Please help me to learn how to love, so that I can live what we sing."

Mello prayed, "Thanks, God, for what this band is teaching me about myself and about you."

"We love you, God," Trin prayed. "Thanks for choosing us."

We jumped when someone banged on the door.

A deep voice said, "Chosen Girls, it's time."

"It's Mr. Smith Number One," Trin said with a giggle.

As we walked toward the stage, Mr. Smith Number Two said over the microphone, "I'm pleased to present ... the Chosen Girls!"

The noise of the applause and cheering actually hurt my ears. My heart pounded so hard I thought I might pass out, and I couldn't quit smiling.

Then the gym went dark.

Lamont started the video, but without sound, just like we had planned. It played on a huge screen behind and above us. The crowd got quiet as they watched a single bubble float across the screen and pop. The words

The Chosen Girls

You've Chosen Me

grew until they filled the screen. Our faces showed next, and then the part I hated—the pictures of three nasty demon-things: P. Ride, Rival Ree, and Jealous E.

The next shot showed us in the shed, starting the song.

In the gym, spotlights shone on us. Right on cue with the video, Mello tapped four beats, and we began.

Trin and Mello's voices filled up the whole building. They sounded way cool.

I couldn't wait for the big moment we had planned ... and then it came faster than I expected. It was our second time through the chorus. On the video behind us, the bad guys were creeping onto stage.

Lamont switched the video to sound. We had stayed so perfectly with the video that it didn't miss a beat of the song.

The light guy turned off the spots, and in the pale light from the video screen, we quietly snuck behind the stage.

We ripped off the outfits we had been wearing, to reveal our new white superhero suits underneath. Thanks to Mello, they looked just like the ones from the video.

We each grabbed a sword and shield (all donated by two sweet little brothers) and snuck back to our places.

Just at the moment on-screen when we turned into super-heroes, the spotlights came back on. We held our swords and shields in fighting position, and Mr. Smith Number One released the glitter. It fell softly from the ceiling and shimmered around us as I did a crescent kick, Trin twirled around, and Mello raised her sword high above her head.

The crowd went crazy-wild. They loved it!

While they were still screaming, we dropped our armor and picked up our instruments. Mello tapped out four beats along with the music on the video. Then Lamont cut the sound, and we came back in live.

We seriously rocked.

I wished Makayla and her Snob Mob could see it. I knew she wouldn't believe me if I talked about it in science or PE.

Then I realized it didn't matter. I wasn't part of the Chosen Girls to impress Makayla. And probably—no matter how famous we got—she would always be her snotty self. But hopefully I had grown up enough to treat her the way I wanted to be treated—even if she couldn't be nice back.

Wasn't that what God did for me? He loved me and accepted me even though I didn't deserve it.

We finished out the concert in our superhero suits. I think it helped Mello—kind of like it wasn't even her on stage in front of all those people. She really got serious on the drums. Trin, of course, rocked like she always does.

My dream was coming true. I finally stood playing my guitar in front of hundreds of people. The crowd was way fun—clapping, singing along, screaming at the end of each song. And the rush was just as good as I expected it to be.

But something didn't match up to my daydreams.

The last song of our debut concert was "Love Lessons." I listened to the words and looked at Trin and Mello as they sang.

Let my love grow.
Let my love show
In every word I say.
Help me reach out
Beyond the doubt
And make this world a better place.
Oh, oh, oh!
Let my love grow.
Bridge*:*
'Cause with you
I find my soul.

I can't go wrong.
I'm not afraid.
Keep on teaching me, reaching me,
Telling me, helping me to
Be the person I should be.

Chorus 2:
Let my love grow.
Let my love show
In every deed I do.
Help me reach out
Beyond the doubt.
Open my heart
To follow you . . .
Oh, oh, oh!
Let my love grow.

I realized what was different from my dreams. In all the scheming and planning I'd done, the only thing that mattered was getting more and more famous. Now I knew getting famous wasn't the most important thing. The love I shared with my best friends was more important than anything that might happen in the band's future.

And the love God showed by choosing me was the most important thing of all.

I played the last note.

The lights went out.

The crowd stood up and cheered.

I bowed my head and said a prayer of thanks.

CHECK OUT this excerpt from book three in the Chosen Girls series.

UNPLUGGED

zonderkidz

Created by Beth Michael
Written by Cheryl Crouch

chapter • 1

...

Thursday

Moving to California scared me 'cause in Dallas I knew where I fit. I survived some hard lessons in Dallas.

Like when I invited those girls from ballet to my birthday bash. Two of the coolest girls in school—my friends. Then when Ashlyn didn't show and Jade dissed everything we did at the party, I understood. They were only friends if nobody else was around.

I didn't want to start over in California. But when I got here, I met the best friends ever—Harmony and Mello. I stopped worrying about past mistakes. Soon I even quit pretending I had my act together.

Ohwow! We started our own rock band! Music videos and rock concerts. We're actually in them, instead of just watching. Sure, we had challenges, but I just knew I didn't have to worry about being embarrassed anymore.

But I was wrong.
So wrong.

• • •

"Give me one more run straight through, and then take five," said the sound engineer over the intercom.

I nodded at him through the huge glass window. The soundman, John, sat in the control room, while Mello, Harmony, and I jammed in studio four. Acoustic tiles, wood, and carpeting covered the floors, walls, and even the ceiling of the room. Our friend Lamont made faces at us behind John's back.

"Sweet! I still can't believe we're in a real recording studio," I said, ignoring Lamont as I quickly fine-tuned my electric guitar.

Mello grinned at me from behind her drum set. "I feel like we live here, after yesterday."

"But how cool is this?" Harmony asked, waving her arms at the microphones, headsets, and glass sound-isolation booths surrounding us. She jerked her head at the control room. "And Lamont looks like he's died and gone to heaven. That control room has enough equipment to launch a space shuttle."

John's voice interrupted us. "Anytime you're ready, Chosen Girls."

Mello tapped three beats and we played the intro. I smiled at Harmony, who played a solid bass line, and then nodded at Mello. We came in on the pickup note:

Oh, Chik'n Quik
Chicken on a stick
It's so yummy for your tummy
Everybody loves Chik'n Quik

Mello's alto blended perfectly with my soprano, and Harmony's bass guitar sounded awesome with my electric. Mello ended the jingle with a cymbal crash. Perfect!

"Thanks," John said. "Take a short break. Be ready to go again in five."

Harmony and I stood our guitars on their stands, and Mello grabbed a bottle of water.

"I can't wait to hear us on the radio!" Harmony said.

Mello laughed. "But ... it's a chicken jingle."

Harmony rounded on her. "Most bands would be psyched to have a manager get them a gig like this. You have to start somewhere."

"But we *have* started," Mello answered. "We're on TV. We do concerts. Why do we need a chicken jingle?"

I giggled as I opened a bottle of juice. I agreed with Mello—it did seem a little lame.

"We need to break into radio," Harmony said in her I'm-trying-to-be-patient-with-you voice. "This is how we're going to do it. Plus, this job got us the hookup for our next concert," she added, digging her hand into a bag of chocolate pretzels and peanuts. "You'll see. Even Makayla and the Snob Mob will forget about our botched show in Lewisville." She flounced to the floor and popped a pretzel in her mouth.

"Makayla and the Snob Mob will always be posers, Harmony," I reminded her. "I thought you figured that out."

Lamont bounded in. "You women sound amazing." He reached for some pretzels. "You sold me. I could eat some chicken on a stick right now!"

The door burst open, and a huge man walked in. "I'm Mr. Walling," he announced in a loud bass voice. "Great studio, huh?"

Harmony put her pretzels behind her and jumped up. "The owner of Chik'n Quik?" She stepped toward him, reaching out her right hand. "I'm Harmony Gomez, manager of the Chosen Girls. I'm the one you spoke to on the phone."

"Glad to meet you, Harmony and Chosen Girls," he boomed, pumping Harmony's arm up and down. "I'm thrilled about our agreement." He seemed to fill the room with his large belly and even larger personality.

"We're ready, sir," John said, sticking his head in the door. He looked at us. "I'm going to play that last recording for Mr. Walling, so you've got a few more minutes of break." He left, and Mr. Walling followed him to the control room.

We could see them talking, but we couldn't hear them through the soundproof glass. They got still, listening. Then Mr. Walling said something. John answered him, and Mr. Walling shook his head. He frowned.

"He didn't like it," Mello whispered.

I watched the discussion, wishing I could read lips but thinking it might be good I couldn't.

"That's normal," I said. "People usually have to record like twenty times to get it right."

Mello tapped nervously on her snare. "I don't think we'll get it any better than that. We aced it."

John leaned over and pushed something, and Mr. Walling's voice filled the room. "Beautiful, just beautiful! I loved it!"

John's voice came next. "I told Mr. Walling he's got the studio for the next four hours, if he wants a few more takes. But he says there's no point."

"Do you have any songs you'd like to record?" Mr. Walling asked. "I've paid for the session, so you might as well use it. And I'd like to listen, if I may."

"Sweet!" I answered. "What first?" I looked at Mello and Harmony, not wanting to waste a second.

" 'You've Chosen Me,' " Harmony said. "Our signature song." I nodded, and Mello got us started. Something about the studio brought out the best in us. We rocked. We sang "Love Lessons" next. John had us each play individually too.

When our time ran out, Mr. Walling came in and shook our hands. "We'll see you tomorrow at the grand opening," he said.

"Yes, sir," Harmony agreed. "I put your posters all over town."

Mello asked, "What time do you want us there, Mr. Walling?"

Harmony looked sideways at her and answered, "Grand Opening at five, Chosen Girls in place by four. Right?"

"That's right," Mr. Walling agreed.

"And where is your restaurant?" I asked. Harmony frowned at me. "I just want to be sure," I explained. "After your mistake in Lewisville . . ."

She glared at me, then turned to Mr. Walling and asked, "The fifteen hundred block of Hibiscus, next to the Wash-and-Run, right?"

Mr. Walling beamed at Harmony. "Just beautiful! I'll see you there." He smiled at all of us. "After what I heard today, I'm even more excited about your concert." He started for the door and added, "Don't forget to listen to the radio. The ad starts running tomorrow." His voice trailed away down the hall. "Beautiful."

John came in as we packed up. "I'll mix and balance these recordings, and you can pick up your CD next week," he told us. "I must say, for a start-up band, you record really well. It takes some groups four days to get a single."

I thanked him, and he said, "That session would usually run you $225 an hour. But don't thank me. Thank Mr. Walling."

As the door closed behind him, Harmony added, "You can also thank your awesome manager. I told you this was a good gig."

...

Friday

We got to Chik'n Quik at three-thirty on Friday.

"I told you we didn't need to leave straight from school," Harmony griped as she hauled an amp out of Mom's Suburban.

I grabbed another amp. "Hey, better safe than sorry," I responded. "If we want to be a real band, we can't afford to be late. Or go to the wrong location."

"I know the location, Trin," Harmony huffed.

Mello stepped between us. "So Mr. Walling wants us to wear our superhero stuff?" she interrupted. "For the whole concert? Why don't we switch during 'You've Chosen Me,' like we usually do?"

"Yeah," Lamont agreed. "The superhero thing doesn't make sense without the video. It explains where your power comes from."

"I guess I can ask," Harmony answered, heading for the flatbed trailer that would be our stage. "But he wanted to know if we'd be willing to do the whole concert in costume, and I said okay. It seemed like a small thing for what he's paying us. I guess he thinks our super suits are cool."

"Way cool," I said, following her. I put the amp on the edge of the stage and waved an imaginary sword around. "Don't you wish just putting the suit on gave you superpowers?"

"I'd wear mine every day," Harmony agreed with a smile.

Lamont put the soundboard down. "Sorry, women. No power in the suits." He looked around. The stage backed up to a small lawn covered in brilliant green grass, tropical flowers, and palms. To the right, cars cruised by on Hibiscus Drive. "This is a great place for the stage. Right by the main drag. Everyone who passes will know something's going on."

Mello said, "I can't believe I'm doing this."

"It's good for you," I answered. "Little by little, you're over-coming your shyness—breaking out of your shell."

"Little by little?" she asked. "More like you went after my shell with a sledgehammer!"

We got our equipment hooked up and ran through sound checks. Then we grabbed the bags with our costumes in them. "Now, aren't you glad we're early?" I asked. "We have time to get dressed and do our hair."

Mello sighed and said, "Trin, your hair already looks great."

"Same to you, Miss Elegance," I answered with a smile.

Mr. Walling met us on the other side of the parking lot, at the door of Chik'n Quik. His bass voice rang out as he said, "Hello, Chosen Girls. Hello, Lamont! I see you found the stage. Beautiful. Come on in and look around." He held the door for us. "What do you think?"

I looked around. It looked like any other fast-food restaurant. "I ... uh ... like the color of your seat covers," I offered.

"Yes, thank you," he answered. "Beautiful."

We headed for the restroom.

Mr. Walling called, "Wait. I have your costumes in the back."

I held up my bag. "No, we've got them here," I corrected. But he was gone.

He came back with a huge box. "Wait till you see these," he said, putting the box on a table. "I ordered three of them from headquarters, and I'm so pleased. You'll stop traffic — no questions asked." He opened the box and reached in.

And pulled out a chicken suit.

• • •

Standing onstage, I looked through the hole cut in the beak of my suit. A few cars had already parked, and people laughed and pointed as they came toward us. More and more cars pulled in.

The chicken head I wore was thick enough to be hot, but not thick enough to block the sounds of horns honking on Hibiscus Drive. More than one guy yelled, "Hey, Chicks! Lookin' good!"

Embarrassed, I looked down at my feet. That didn't help. Red chicken claws were there where my ultracool high-heeled boots belonged.

Harmony wisely avoided eye contact. Her bright yellow beak faced straight ahead as we ran through final checks, so I could only see her white feathers and skinny yellow chicken legs.

"At least no one can recognize us." Mello's weak voice came from the direction of her drums, behind me.

I turned to look at her. "Mello, thanks to our overeager manager, signs all over town say 'Chosen Girls to perform at Grand Opening.' Everyone knows it's us."

"So what do you want me to do?" Harmony hissed. "He's paying us. He gave us a free recording session."

Mr. Walling strode across the parking lot toward us, flashing a huge smile and a double thumbs-up. He came onstage and grabbed my microphone.

"Thanks for coming out to our grand opening," he told the gathering crowd. "Please enjoy free samples of our delicious Chik'n Quik chicken on a stick while you listen to the music of the best new group in Southern California: the Chosen Girls!" He turned to us. "Open with the jingle!"

He walked offstage and we started in. I was singing, "It's so yummy for your tummy," when I first saw them in the crowd.

Makayla and the Snob Mob.

• • •

After the concert, Mom dropped us at the shed in Mello's backyard. I don't know why we call it the shed. It's more like an apartment or a studio. It's got everything—a couch, TV, plenty of room to jam. It's even decorated with real art and throw pillows that match the curtains.

We unloaded our equipment. But that wasn't all we unloaded.

"Unbelievable!" I shouted at Harmony. "You are the only person who could mess this up so royally." I put my electric down and flopped onto the couch.

"Do you think I enjoyed it?" she yelled back. She threw an armload of extension cords down. "Humiliating myself in front of Makayla and company? *Again!*"

"Forget about the Snob Mob. Half of Hopetown was there," I wailed.

"Look on the bright side," Lamont said, carrying in a drum.

Mello put a snare in the corner and glared at him. "There is no bright side, Lamont."

"But there is," he insisted. "Remember what Trin said before the concert? Based on your costumes today, I'd say Mello isn't the only one who broke out of her shell." He slapped his thigh. "Get it? Chickens? Eggs?"

I rolled my eyes. "So *not* funny, Lamont," I told him. "Harmony, how many times do you expect us to put up with this? I'm not used to being humiliated."

"Stick around," Mello said. "You might *get* used to it."

Harmony looked at me, then at Lamont, and then at Mello. No one said anything.

Harmony blinked and took a deep breath like she didn't want to cry. Then she turned and stomped out.

Lamont followed her.

"I'm with you, Trin," Mello said. "I mean, Harmony's like a sister to me. Has been since second grade. But I can't handle any more of her messes." She sat next to me and put her head in her hands. "What we need is a manager who can actually manage." She looked at me. "I bet you'd be a good manager."

I let out a big breath and shook my head.

. . .

We needed to regroup, so we met at Java Joint later.

I apologized to Harmony for my attitude. Mello clued in and said she was sorry too. Lamont didn't make any more smart remarks, and it looked like we would be okay.

Then the Snob Mob came in. Makayla pointed to us and yelled, "Look! My favorite rock band: the Chicken Girls."

Thankfully, they got their drinks to go.

Harmony started bawling. "I'm such a loser. Why do you guys even let me hang with you? I wish ..." She stopped to wipe her nose on her sleeve. "I wish I could just leave the country!"

I looked into her red, swollen eyes and yelled, "That's it!"

They all looked at me.

I flashed them my biggest smile and said, "It's perfect. Exactly what we need. Let's go to Russia!"

Unplugged

Book Three • Softcover • ISBN 0-310-71269-6

The band lands a fantastic opportunity to travel to Russia, but the "international tour," as they dub it, brings out Trinity's take-charge personality. Almost too confidently, she tries to control fundraising efforts and the tour to avoid another mess by Harmony. But cultural challenges, band member clashes, and some messes of her own convince Trinity she's not really in charge after all. God is. And his plan includes changed lives, deepened faith, and improved relationships with her mom and friends.

zonderkidz

Solo Act

Book Four • Softcover • ISBN 0-310-71270-X

Melody needs some downtime—and the summer youth retreat will really
hit the spot! But a last-minute crisis at camp means an opportunity for
the band to lead worship every morning, plus headline the camp's big
beach concert and go to camp for free. Too busy and unhappy, Melody
makes some selfish choices that result in the girls getting lost, sunburned,
in trouble, and embarrassed. Can she pull out of the downward spiral
before she ruins camp—and the band—completely?

Available November 2007 at your local bookstore!

Big Break

Book Five • Softcover • ISBN 0-310-71271-8

The Chosen Girls are back! As opportunities for the band
continue to grow, Harmony can't resist what she sees
as a big break ... and what could be better than
getting signed by an agent?

Sold Out

Book Six • Softcover • ISBN 0-310-71272-6

Dedicated to proving herself to others, Trinity gets involved in organizing the school talent show. Before she knows it, she accepts a dare from Chosen Girls' rival band to be decided by the outcome of a commercial audition.

Available November 2007 at your local bookstore!

Overload

Book Seven • Softcover • ISBN 0-310-71273-4

Melody discovers a latent talent for leadership that she never
knew she had. When she begins a grief recovery group for kids
like her, she loses her focus on the work God is doing
through the Chosen Girls.

zonder**kidz**

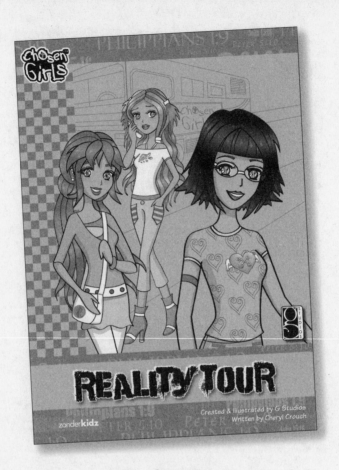

Reality Tour

Book Eight • Softcover • ISBN 0-310-71274-2

When the Chosen Girls go on their first multi-city tour in a
borrowed RV, Harmony's messiness almost spoils their final show.
What's worse, she almost blows her opportunity to witness to
her cousin Lucinda.

zonder**kidz**

zonder**kidz**.

We want to hear from you. Please send your comments
about this book to us in care of zreview@zondervan.com. Thank you.

Grand Rapids, MI 49530
www.zonderkidz.com

ZONDERVAN.com/
AUTHORTRACKER
follow your favorite authors